"I hate y

"I don't care," Vero said, and that she was still lying to him, to herself, made his voice rough then, brutal even. "And I don't care that you don't want to marry me. Because, Princess Bettina, in four weeks' time, you and I are going to be married whether you like it or not." He stared down steadily into her huge dazed eyes. "You know, your father offered me a plot of land out in the hills as part of your dowry, but I'm happy to take that kiss as a down payment."

She sucked in a breath.

"Get out—"

Her face was flushed with an anger that should have made her look ugly but instead highlighted the luminosity of her skin.

"Don't worry, I'm going." Without bothering to straighten his shirt, he strolled toward the door. He stopped beside it, his hand resting lightly on the handle, and turned to face her. "But I believe your father has arranged a dinner to celebrate our engagement, so we'll meet again tomorrow evening, Your Royal Highness. You can be sure of that."

Louise Fuller was a tomboy who hated pink and always wanted to be the prince—not the princess! Now she enjoys creating heroines who aren't pretty pushovers but are strong, believable women. Before writing for Harlequin, she studied literature and philosophy at university, then worked as a reporter on her local newspaper. She lives in Royal Tunbridge Wells with her impossibly handsome husband, Patrick, and their six children.

Books by Louise Fuller

Harlequin Presents

The Italian's Runaway Cinderella
Maid for the Greek's Ring
Their Dubai Marriage Makeover
Returning for His Ruthless Revenge
Her Diamond Deal with the CEO

Hot Winter Escapes

One Forbidden Night in Paradise

Behind the Billionaire's Doors...

Undone in the Billionaire's Castle

The Diamond Club

Reclaimed with a Ring

Ruthless Rivals

Boss's Plus-One Demand
Nine-Month Contract

Visit the Author Profile page
at Harlequin.com for more titles.

ROYAL RING OF REVENGE

LOUISE FULLER

PRESENTS

Harlequin®
PRESENTS™

ISBN-13: 978-1-335-21905-3

Recycling programs for this product may not exist in your area.

Royal Ring of Revenge

Harlequin Enterprises ULC
22 Adelaide St. West, 41st Floor
Toronto, Ontario M5H 4E3, Canada
www.Harlequin.com

Printed in U.S.A.

ROYAL RING OF REVENGE

CHAPTER ONE

BETTY'S FATHER WAS waiting for her in one of the private lounges that offered both afternoon sunlight and unparalleled views of Morroello and its famous brick-built *campanile*. She stopped the requisite three feet away, gave a small, bobbing curtsey and then, stepping closer, brushed first one papery cheek, then the other, with her lips. Theirs was not an affectionate relationship, but convention required that she kiss her father and so that was what she did.

'Papà—'

'Bettina—'

He gestured towards one of the silk-covered armchairs that her mother had chosen during her last redecoration of the palace. The silk was pale peach with tiny embroidered blooms and delicate green foliage to symbolise the national flower of Malaspina, the bergamot. It was exquisite and impractical, a bit like her mother.

'Is everything all right? Are you feeling—?'

'I'm fine.' Her father waved his hand as if

he were dismissing a particularly irritating fly. 'Leave us.'

As the uniformed footman retreated from the room, Betty sat down, folding her knees sideways and sitting up straight. Her father was looking at her critically. 'You've caught the sun.'

She felt her cheeks burn then, just as if the sun's rays had touched her there. In addition to her sunny nature and sweet smile, her younger sister, Bella, had been born with the kind of enviable smooth, golden skin that rarely if ever burned. Betty, on the other hand, required the thickest, highest SPF so that she looked as if she had slathered herself in white emulsion paint. At best, a day sitting in the sun would result in a smattering of freckles on her shoulders and along her cheekbones, but more likely her skin would turn a vivid and painful scarlet before peeling to reveal new, even paler skin.

It was one of the downsides of being a redhead.

There were others, the most significant of which was the fact that neither of her parents shared her fiery hair and pale complexion and so there had been questions asked both in private and in public about her paternity. Jokes made in the media at her father's expense, which he hated of course. Which was maybe why he hated her.

Her throat tightened, clamping around her breath so that it was suddenly hard to swallow.

He didn't actually hate her, she thought dully. Hating anything would require an intensity of emotion that was not simpatico with being the Prince of Malaspina, so his frustration and fury were suppressed because her father never forgot, even for a moment, that he was a prince, and the ruler of the principality, a king in all but name.

She could never forget it either, or that she was a princess and the heir apparent to the throne. Since childhood, she had been drilled to appear dutiful and compliant. No whisper of scandal or rumours of even the slightest indiscretion had ever been attached to her.

But it had come at a price.

She glanced over to where her father sat in his wing armchair, his cufflinks gleaming at his wrists, his cravat loosely knotted beneath his smooth face.

No, he didn't hate her. It was worse than that. He was disappointed by her.

Had been disappointed by her since she emerged from the womb, not the longed-for son but a daughter with the wrong colour hair.

Wrong everything.

'You should be more careful.'

I was careful, she thought. I am always careful. But it was never enough for either of her parents. She was never enough, had disappointed both of them since conception when her mother had been horribly ill during the pregnancy to the point that she'd had to be hospitalised.

Her father shifted in his seat. 'Remember that you don't have your sister's skin.'

How could she not remember? She was reminded of it at least once a day.

No doubt it was just the burn of the wind from driving back to the city with the soft top down, but she wouldn't tell her father that. Despite having agreed to her doing so, he disliked her driving herself. To him it smacked of individuality and any sign of self-expression was a slippery slope as far as he was concerned and could easily lead to the wanton excesses of his father, Frederico, who had abdicated the throne a decade ago following a series of damaging revelations about his private life.

'I know, Papà, but Bella wanted to have a picnic before she went to Switzerland, so we went up to the waterfall.'

'So I understand.' Prince Vittorio nodded. 'It's good to mark these transitions.'

Betty held her father's gaze. Since the operation, he had been markedly weaker and usually he looked tired in the afternoons, but today he seemed more focused.

'Would you say she seems ready for the next stage of her life?'

'Definitely.' She nodded quickly. It had taken

LOUISE FULLER   **11**

a lot of persuasion, but the Prince had finally, grudgingly, agreed that Bella could take a year abroad in Switzerland, and she knew that Bella would be devastated if their father changed his mind.

'She's grown up a lot in the last year. She is much more aware of her role and she's already thinking about the future of Malaspina.'

That wasn't strictly true. All Bella was really interested in was her twenty-first birthday party. They had discussed the guest list and the entertainment options and, most important of all, Bella's outfit, at length. But her father didn't need to know that.

She'd always had a maternal relationship with her younger sister and since her mother's death, that was even truer. But, remembering her own restrictive adolescence, she had tried to be kinder, more understanding. Which meant that, unlike her, Bella had friends and a social life. She went to parties—with her close protection officers, of course—and she had a strict curfew. But she was having fun as any normal twenty-year-old would, and should.

There was a pause as her father glanced away to the picture-postcard view of his principality and stared at it fixedly as if he suddenly needed to reassure himself that it was still there.

'You asked to see me, Papà…' she prompted.

Not asked. She had been summoned, pulled away from the one afternoon off she'd had in months.

He nodded.

'Is it about Bella?' She silently offered up a prayer.

Please don't let him have changed his mind.

'No. It's about your grandfather.' His mouth tightened. 'He called me this morning.'

She stared at him, her pulse leapfrogging over itself. Ten years ago, the details about Frederico's extramarital affairs had been largely contained by the sympathetic Malaspinian media, but outside the country the Internet had fizzed with kiss-and-tell stories from his mistresses and former staff.

'He called me. To warn me.'

'About what?' Her body stiffened. Surely everything that could have been said or printed about Frederico's affairs was already well documented.

She let her gaze move infinitesimally to the window to where a trio of crescent-shaped swallows were darting joyously through the warm sunlight.

Lucky swallows, she thought, watching them somersault through the sky. They got to leave when things got hard.

Her father turned towards her now, his face

composed, but his shoulders were quivering with frustration and suppressed fury. 'That woman of his, the one he married. She's pregnant.'

She blinked. Swallowed. Tried to breathe through her shock.

'That's—' She hesitated, trying to find a word that could do justice to her own stunned reaction and yet not do anything to exacerbate the vein pulsing in her father's forehead. 'That's unfortunate, but what Nonno does is no longer our concern—'

The Prince pursed his lips into a familiar moue of exasperation. 'If you truly believe that then you are either naive or short-sighted. Of course it is our concern. Your grandfather is the Prince Emeritus of Malaspina, and he is having a child. I'm well aware he has no claim on the throne, but it will send shock waves through our country. There will be questions asked. We need to have answers. What we can't do is take anything for granted. Nothing is certain if the people take against you, as you well know from the experience of your mother's family.'

Betty said nothing. Her mother's family had lost their throne ninety years ago and been living in exile ever since. Their banishment had shaped her grandmother's and mother's lives, lacing every day with a bitterness and paranoia that were as exhausting as they were relentless.

In fact, that was true of every member of her family except her disgraced grandfather, who had escaped the shroud of despair and was now living freely and happily on the other side of the world.

'I do know, Papà,' she agreed.

'We need to offer a stronger narrative, one that will secure our future. Your future. And as a matter of some urgency. Which is why I asked to see you.'

Her father paused, and for no reason she shivered.

'My future?'

She might as well have asked, 'What future?'

Unlike former widowed princesses in previous generations, she was not required to wear black for an indefinite period, but despite having returned to her official duties just two weeks after her late husband's funeral she hadn't been encouraged to do much more than that.

He nodded. His blue eyes held hers. The Marchetta blue eyes that had been passed down through generations to Bella but bypassed Betty. 'I am aware that you had plans. Plans that had to take second place to the needs of the crown. But I think now would be a good time to revisit those plans.'

'What plans?' Since her mother's death, she had simply stepped into her shoes, taking on her roles as the patron of various charities. It meant

she had less time for herself. She stared at him,
trying to follow the route he was taking to the
end point, the final destination.

'Why, marriage, of course.' Her father frowned.

Something kicked against her ribs so that her
body jerked backwards into the upholstery.

Marriage?

No. She tried to say the word out loud, but her
mouth wouldn't form the shape of it, but then it
had no understanding of how to do so because
she had never said no to her father. Even when he
had told her that he had found her a husband nine
years ago, just a week after she and Vero had broken up. If you could break up from something that
had only existed for real inside one person's head.

She had been twenty, the same age as Bella
now.

Her eyes flickered to the gold band on her
finger.

It was hard to believe she had ever been that
young. That woman who had spoken vows in the
cathedral in front of a carefully curated congregation felt like someone half remembered from
a dream or a novel. Had she been like Bella? She
hadn't been as naive as her sister, for sure. By then
her heart had been broken, her dreams crushed.
She had risked everything for love and for what?

An ambitious young man without scruples.
Or a heart.

No wonder her father had been disappointed. Her mother, too. It had been a whole new level of disappointment. And shock, enough to cause the stroke from which her mother never fully recovered. It had all been downplayed by the Palace but not forgotten by her. Watching the panic in her mother's eyes as she struggled to speak would stay with her for ever.

That stroke was why she had agreed to marry Alberto. At least being married was one box ticked.

Alberto had been ten years older than her. He had been a loud, boring, humourless man without charm. But he had been a prince. That was all that had mattered to her parents.

And at that point nothing had mattered to her. Most days she had woken up desperate to go back to sleep. If she could have done so she would have stayed asleep for ever. No prince could have woken her with a kiss.

But then she hadn't been in love with a prince.

More importantly, the man she'd loved hadn't been in love with her.

And so she'd married Alberto, who also hadn't loved her despite the fairy-tale hype spun by the Malaspinian media. He had worn a uniform. Trousers with a side stripe, a jacket with gold buttons and an array of medals. And he had been tall. But aside from that he had been entirely average with receding dark hair and that air of superficial courtesy that had been a mask for his stunted intellect and emotional immaturity.

Having a title of equal grandeur had been their only common ground, and after the honeymoon, with its excruciatingly awkward and unsatisfying wedding night, they had settled into a dull equilibrium that had been bearable because Alberto had not expected anything of her. Not wanted anything from her or, rather, anything more from her than her blue blood.

And she hadn't wanted anything from him.

She certainly hadn't wanted him to die. But then his yacht had been caught at sea in a storm and he'd been swept overboard and suddenly she was a widow in her twenties. Overnight she was single.

But not free.

Except, apparently, to remarry.

Lifting her chin, she met her father's blue gaze.

'It's very kind of you to think of me, Papà, but I don't want to marry again.'

'Nonsense. You are a young woman. More importantly, you are a princess. You need to provide an heir, a legitimate heir to the throne of Malaspina, and for that to happen you need to be married.'

It was blindingly obvious that was the case. She had known it when she'd married Alberto.

Known it still when she'd buried him. To be relevant, to secure its future, unlike the other monarchies of Europe that had fizzled out, the House of Marchetta needed heirs, but she had simply blocked that fact out.

'And I did marry. I married a man I didn't love who didn't love me.'

'Love!' Her father tutted. 'A monarchy is not sustained by love, Bettina. It is sustained by pragmatism. By treaties and alliances and by an acceptance that the needs of the crown take precedence over the wishes of any one individual. For the House of Marchetta to retain its position, sacrifices have to be made.'

'And I have made them,' she protested, but her voice sounded weak and ineffectual.

'And you will continue to do so. However, in this instance, you will only be required to do what you would have done of your own volition if your mother and I hadn't intervened.'

She could feel the adrenaline pulsing through her body.

There was only one time that she had done anything of her own volition. Only that would mean—

'I don't understand,' she lied, because she did understand. But after so long keeping it separate from her life, she just didn't want to believe it, to accept that this was happening to her, here, now. That her father, her own father, had gone and opened that chest, letting out the past with all its messiness and pain and humiliation.

'I've had an offer for your hand in marriage and, for the good of your family, for your country, you need to accept it.'

She cleared her throat. 'An offer from whom?'

It was a rhetorical question. She already knew the answer but until her father spoke his name out loud it wasn't real.

'Vero Farnese.'

The floor rippled beneath her feet.

Vero with his dark green eyes that were the exact same colour as the pine trees that edged the hills around Malaspina. Vero with his high cheekbones and hard, flawless profile. He might not have stuck around, but he had stayed in her head.

'Why him?' It didn't make any sense. Nine years ago, Vero wouldn't have made the long longlist of potential suitors.

'Because he asked,' her father said tersely. 'And his situation has changed. Improved.'

She wanted to laugh. Because that was something of an understatement. There might be an ocean between them now, but she would have to have been living under a rock on a different planet not to know that Vero's situation had changed, unquestionably and dramatically.

Nine years ago, he had been the son of the family chauffeur living in a cottage on the estate with his parents.

Now his company was a household name. The cars he designed and produced were changing the way people drove. Oh, and he was one of the richest men in the world.

'But we don't need his money.'

Her father tilted his head on one side as he always did when he was displeased with his eldest daughter. 'Don't be childish, Bettina. You know how expensive it has been to settle your grandfather's debts. Signor Farnese is a wealthy man, and he is offering a not insignificant amount of money for your hand.' Her father exhaled as if the scent of non-inherited wealth was offensive to him. 'Naturally, I would prefer someone of royal blood—'

'But he's the son of our former chauffeur. He has no bloodline. Surely you're concerned about that, Papà.'

'He has no pedigree. Or not the sort that matters. He's something of a mongrel—' The Prince smiled coldly. 'But successful monarchies like ours understand the importance not just of maintaining traditions and protocol but of embracing the mood of the times. Marrying a commoner will show that we are open to the changing world. Plus, Signor Farnese has a close connection with the family.'

Close connection.

She felt suddenly sick. Except it hadn't been close, she thought, Vero's deep voice filling her head as she fast-forwarded through their last conversation, out by the garages. It was an appearance of closeness. She wasn't his heart's desire, but simply a means to an end. Only he was her first lover, her first love, and she had got so lost in the intimacy and intensity of sex that it had blurred her senses, made her lose all common sense.

'He grew up in Malaspina, which will play well with the people. And he is here, unlike your grandfather.'

It was one of the things her father did to distance himself from the man who had cast such a long shadow over his life. Not referring to him as his father. Making it Bettina's problem. But right now, she had bigger problems.

Like being married off to a man she hated.

Her father was getting to his feet, using the armrest to propel himself to standing, and she stood too, if only because it gave her more of a chance to flee from this nightmarish conversation.

'We need to get ahead of this story. Otherwise, we will look weak.' He looked suddenly exhausted, and she knew why. Her mother's family, older, grander than the House of Marchetta, had been ousted from their throne, pushed into exile after a series of scandals and allegations of corruption had left them weak and isolated.

Nobody wanted a weak monarch. That was as true now as it had ever been.

She felt her whole body tense. Vero. His name meant true, but he had lied to her, used her, manipulated her, manipulated her trust.

Her fingers tightened into fists. She wouldn't marry him. She couldn't. It would break her, and he had already done that once.

'What makes you think his offer is real?' she said stiffly. 'I mean, why would he want to marry me? Or have you forgotten that nine years ago you sacked his father and evicted his whole family from their home?'

Saying it aloud made her shiver inside. She hadn't seen Vero after that had happened but his anger when she'd ended things had been coldly absolute. So why was he back? Why did he want her?

Leaning forward to press a button on a small marble topped table, her father held her gaze. 'Of course, it's real. What man doesn't want to marry a princess?'

As he walked slowly towards the door that led to his private salon she swayed slightly. She felt sick, but it was just a horrible coincidence. Her father couldn't have known that Vero had asked her almost exactly the same question nine years ago.

It was a question that had haunted her dreams ever since. She could still remember her panic and confusion and then that hot rush of shame as she'd understood that Vero was interested in her title, not her. There was a knock on the other door, the one through which she had entered the room.

Her father turned, his face lined but composed in the afternoon sunlight, and she knew that for him the matter was resolved.

'But if you don't believe me, ask him yourself. Ah, Giuliano—' He turned towards the man in his dark green uniform who had appeared to hover discreetly next to the wall. 'Is the car ready? I should like to leave for Arduino now—'

'But, Papà—'

It was too late. She stared across the sunlit room as the door closed behind him, her heart jumping against her ribs. And then she heard the other door open…

'Your Royal Highness—'

She turned, her legs moving slowly as if it was she, not her father, who was nearly eighty. The footman ducked his chin and stepped back smartly away from the door.

'Signor Vero Farnese.'

And then she felt the air snap to attention, and he was in the room, and she had thought she knew what misery was, but she had to dig her nails into the palm of her hand to redistribute the shattering pain of seeing him again. It was impossible, overwhelming.

He was overwhelming in that dark suit.

Devastating. Powerful. Male.

It was the first time she had seen him in anything other than jeans and a T-shirt. No, that wasn't quite true. She had seen pictures of him online. Pictures that had come up when she'd typed in his name during those occasional moments of self-pity and weakness late at night when the darkness had made her feel as if she were buried alive.

She'd told herself that he would have a stylist now. But the truth was he didn't need a stylist. He never had.

He stopped and gave a small bow and a shiver ran through her, tightening her skin around her bones so that it felt as if she were turning to stone beneath his scrutiny. She felt painfully self-conscious. Was he assessing her, seeing if she had changed for the better? The answer to that question made her so aware of herself that it was hard to breathe, much less appraise him in return.

'Your Royal Highness—'

Had he called her that before?

Maybe, when the grown-ups were there. But never when they were alone. Then he had called her *'dolcezza'*—sweetness.

Her stomach was a snake twisting itself into knots and she put a hand on the back of her father's armchair to steady herself. Behind Vero, the door was closing and nine years, two months, three weeks and five days after he had broken her heart—broken her, truthfully—she was alone again with Vero Farnese.

Had it been a different kind of reunion she might have stepped forward then and embraced him and said something like, *You haven't changed a bit.*

Her blood pulsed sluggishly in her veins. Outside, the noise of the traffic seemed more distant. The curtains that had been fluttering in the light summer breeze stilled. Even the swallows were silent.

Now she looked at him.

But he had changed. The soft-mouthed boy who had ruined her for other men with his kisses had hardened into something almost sculptural. His jawline was smooth like polished marble. A sketch of his body would be all strong lines and aggressive curves, a flagrantly masculine silhouette. Because now he was a man. And though she had probably seen more beautiful, sexier men in the nine years since they last met, she really couldn't remember when.

She couldn't remember much of anything at all. Her brain was just a mush of disconnected thoughts that made no sense. Up until this moment she had been almost proud of how she'd dealt with the past. She would have told herself, told anyone, if they'd bothered to ask, that she was over him.

Now that felt naive, childish even, like something Bella would say.

Somewhere in the palace, a door slammed, and it made her jump, the noise jolting through her body and forcing unexpected tears into her eyes.

Vero's green eyes narrowed onto her face, and she felt suddenly horribly exposed and then furious with herself.

I'm not crying because of you, she wanted to snap at him.

Instead, tamping down her anger and misery in a way that would have earned one of her mother's rare nods of approval, she said coolly, 'I don't know why you've chosen to come back now after all these years, but you've had your fun, and now you can leave.'

A flood of panic washed over her as he moved then, and it took every ounce of willpower she had not to turn and yank open the windows and hurl herself into the warm Malaspinian sunlight.

'Leave?'

She squared her shoulders as he stopped in front of her, his green eyes cool and narrowed on her face, his gaze so familiar and yet also the gaze of a stranger.

He was quiet for a beat, staring at her as if she were a piece of art he didn't understand, and then he said softly, 'Oh, I'm not going anywhere, Princess Bettina.'

She bit the inside of her cheek as he took another step closer.

'As for the fun…' He paused, his gaze moving slowly down over her body, returning to hover on her quivering mouth. 'That hasn't started yet.'

CHAPTER TWO

IT HAD BEEN a long and uncomfortable flight from New York. There were storms above the Atlantic and the turbulence had left his normally tranquil stewards reaching for the sides of the private jet. But it had been worth it, Vero Farnese thought, to watch that flutter of panic in Betty's grey eyes.

Nine years ago, those eyes had mesmerised him. Looking into them was like walking in that fine mist that sometimes rolled in from the sea near his beach house in Malibu. He had been disorientated, blind and helpless. Willingly so.

Like some supplicant offering himself up as a sacrifice. That was what love did. It made you stupid and vulnerable. Which was why he'd always been so careful, so careful, to keep his distance.

His father had taught him that. Not Tommasino, the man who had raised him as his own, but his birth father, the Duke, who had disowned him before he was even born. The man who had discarded his mother after a short affair and paid for her silence so that his true identity had been known to only four people on the planet. Three now.

That silence had been a heavy burden for his parents to carry, but they had carried it uncomplainingly until he had discovered his birth certificate and demanded answers, and in doing so brought fear into their lives.

Having his birth father in the same headspace as Betty made his shoulders stretch back so far that it felt as if the bones would break.

But then, between them they had broken everything else, so why should his shoulder bones be exempt?

'Is that a threat?'

The warm light caught on her cheekbones, highlighting their sharpness. He wasn't a connoisseur of beauty. Yes, he liked a well-cut suit, and he had a weakness for a raked, low-slung, mid-engine performance car, although he didn't like to classify it as such. But he didn't collect art or decorative 'objects' and his homes were starkly decorated, functional spaces.

And Betty shouldn't be beautiful. Taken separately, her features were unremarkable and yet she had that same mesmeric effect on him as *La Gioconda* had on the millions of people who swarmed to the Louvre in Paris just to see her enigmatic smile.

Only Betty wasn't smiling. Her mouth was pressed together into a line that screamed irritation and it shouldn't have looked attractive, but he found himself noticing that fullness of her upper lip and the pinkness of both lips so that, briefly, he lost track of what they were talking about. That mouth...

He dragged his thoughts back to heel and shrugged.

'I don't know. Are you feeling threatened?'

Her look was excoriating. 'By you?' She shook her head, then frowned, feigning thought. 'A better adjective would be bored.'

She meant every word. Unfortunately, that message hadn't been passed on to her body, he thought, his eyes arrowing in on the pulse jerking in her throat. Her hands were shaking slightly too.

Just as they used to when she ran them over his body.

He sucked in a breath, reeling slightly as his brain unhelpfully offered up an image of Betty naked, straddling him, her graceful fingers tracing the contours of his abdomen.

It had been one of the many confusing, contradictory, compelling things about her. She had always been the first to touch but she was shy about initiating sex, almost as if she needed permission to take what she wanted. He'd had to take things up a notch, licking into her mouth or cupping her face, but once he'd done so it had been as if a switch had flipped, and she'd caught fire like a match striking against a flint.

And he had burned beneath her touch. She had made him feel precious and powerful and necessary.

But, of course, the opposite had been true. He had been disposable and he'd had no power over her. She had simply and briefly given him permission to use her body and in exchange she had wanted to use his.

Gritting his teeth, he blanked out the memory of their naked bodies moving on the sunsoaked bed in his room above the garages, and let his eyes drift over her twitching pulse down to where her nipples were clearly visible against the thin silk of her blouse.

'Oh, I don't think you find me boring, Princess. In fact, I'd lay odds that this is the most stimulation you've had in a long time.'

Her eyes blazed but, probably because she knew that it would only give weight to his claim, she bit back whatever protest was rising in her throat, took a step back from him and walked pointedly across the room to the window.

For a moment or two, he took advantage of

that viewpoint and let his gaze roam over her light curves. Only when he'd had his fill and when it became clear that she was ignoring him, did he say, 'You know pretending I'm not here is not going to change anything. Your father and I have already made the decision—'

Betty turned then, goaded, as he'd known she would be, into acknowledging his presence. 'Yes, the two of you.' There was a flush of colour across her cheekbones and a lost note in her voice that made his breath catch. 'Only it isn't your decision to make, it's mine.'

Wrong, he thought, replaying his conversation with Prince Vittorio.

In any other situation, he would have agreed with her. But truthfully the decision had been made by proxy when her unrepentant scandal magnet of a grandfather had impregnated his new wife and looted the Marchetta family's private accounts to fund his lifestyle.

But he wasn't here to persuade Betty of that fact. Her father could make her see sense.

'So, this part of the palace is where you actually live. I always wondered what it was like.'

The faintest flush, like a drop of cochineal, spread slowly across her cheekbones, and he felt another stab of satisfaction at seeing her so discomfited.

To give himself a little longer to enjoy that

sensation, he glanced around the exquisite sitting room. Like most royal residences, the Prince's Palace of Malaspina was mostly given over to state rooms that served as meeting spaces for foreign dignitaries and other guests. These rooms were also open to the public for selected dates during the year when crowds of curious tourists eagerly made their way from the banqueting hall to the throning room, gazing in awe at the gilded mirrors and the grand curving staircase and even grander old masters and the elaborate ceilings with their plaster figurines.

But this was no state room. His green eyes lingered on a portrait of Betty's mother, the late Princess Henrietta.

This particular sitting room was in one of the private apartments that had never been open to the public. Apartments that were reserved for the Marchetta family and the rare, chosen few who were deemed worthy enough to receive an invitation into the inner sanctum.

Which, up until now, hadn't been him, he thought, his jaw tightening.

Nine years ago, when he had been merely the penniless son of the chauffeur, the closest he had got to these particular rooms was standing on the gravel path outside the door to the staff entrance.

'Yes. But only some of the time.'

Coming out of anyone else's mouth, that light,

decisive way she spoke would have sounded like flirting. But he knew better. He knew that it was the voice of a princess used to giving instructions to be followed.

He felt anger flare up inside him again.

Anger with her for leading him away from that path he had chosen through the woods. But mostly anger with himself for being led around like some puppy on a leash.

He should have known then that Betty had simply been curious, not committed. It was, after all, a story as old as time. Uptown girl wanting to see how the other half lived. A princess swapping her crown for a baseball cap and sneaking out of the palace to play with the hired help.

Something rose up in his chest as he remembered their 'secret' meetings and the cloak and dagger way they had communicated.

At the time he hadn't questioned it. In part, he'd found it an aphrodisiac. In the same way, the randomness of the encounters had left him in a near-constant state of sexual anticipation, because every moment had been filled with the possibility that she might appear. And even when those feelings had tipped over into frustration, he'd simply accepted that it had been necessary in order for them to have a relationship.

Relationship. The word ripped through him like a blade.

There had been no relationship. For Betty, it had been simply a fling. *Un'avventura*, as their Italian neighbours across the border would say. Other little girls dressed up as princesses, but Betty was a princess and had wanted to drive a getaway car or break out of prison. Instead, she had hooked up with a man who was rough enough around the edges to give her that good-girl-gone-bad feeling.

But it had been just a feeling. A fantasy. He might have thought it was the real thing, but all Betty had wanted was to cosplay *Roman Holiday* for one summer and then go back to her life at the palace and marry her prince.

Which was exactly what she'd done.

He felt Betty's gaze on the side of his face, and he was suddenly close to asking her why she had picked him. And why he hadn't been enough.

It wasn't the first time he'd asked himself that question. That had been when he was fifteen years old. Neither child nor man and, like most teenagers, he had been shedding his skin when he discovered the truth about his father.

His jaw tightened. Father, only in the sense that he had impregnated his mother.

But Vero was illegitimate, and as such he was not just irrelevant but an embarrassment.

The Duca di Monte Giusto had been coldly furious at being confronted by living proof of his infidelity. With two sons already, he'd had no need even for a spare. More importantly he'd felt no compulsion to acknowledge a connection with his bastard on any level. There had been words, and then a moment of temper that he regretted still, and always would, because it had hurt the man who had stepped up to be his father. Tommasino had been arrested, then released, but the threat of prison had hung over him, and left his mother terrified and anxious for the rest of her life.

Vero had been escorted from the estate and warned never to return.

And then a decade later, Betty's father had done more or less the same thing. Or his minions had. Men like Prince Vittorio employed people to do their dirty work.

'In the winter months, we stay here in Morroello but in the summer, we spend most weekends in Arduino.' Her grey gaze was darker now, less like mist, more like storm clouds, and he felt the air around him dip just as it had on the plane.

It was less symbolic than the palace in Morroello but the Castello della Arduino's location in the countryside was a neat decision by the sixth Prince of Malaspina to demonstrate to the largely rural population of the country that the monarch had their ear.

That was the thing about royalty. Nothing

was accidental or random. Everything, including marriage, was strategic.

Especially marriage.

It was a lesson he'd taken to heart.

'Of course you do,' he murmured. He had never been there either. During their time together, the Castello had been closed for restoration work. But it wouldn't have made any difference if it hadn't been. There was no reason for the son of the chauffeur to visit the family's holiday retreat. Questions would have been asked and nobody would have liked the answers. He knew that. Moreover, he knew that Betty did too.

Her spine stiffened then, and she tilted back her head and held his gaze and he felt it, that flutter of anticipation that he hadn't felt in so long. Hadn't felt with any woman before or since because her posture was how you knew she was a princess.

That, and her slate-grey eyes. They were things of beauty.

Those eyes locked with his now. 'I don't know if you remember but Morroello can get unbearably hot in July and August—'

'Oh, I remember,' he said softly.

Her pupils flared and he knew why. Knew that she was remembering that summer nine years ago. It had been so hot that the surface of the roads had turned to liquid. But the tar wasn't the only thing that had melted that summer.

His blood thundered in his veins, his body tensing painfully hard as he pictured those afternoons in the rooms above the garage. He could practically smell the motor oil and the leather. And her. Not just the perfume she wore but the scent of her warm, damp skin sinking into his, her breath melting in his mouth, and her hand gripping his arms, fingers biting into the muscle as she came apart on top of him.

A flood of heat surged through him, violent and heady, and his skin felt suddenly electric, and his voice was hoarse as he replied.

'I remember everything.'

Her chin snapped up and their eyes collided as a quivering silence stretched out to the gilded edges of the room.

'Then you'll know to take the left exit at the Zafferano roundabout to reach the airport,' she said at last. 'I'm sorry you had a wasted trip, Signor Farnese, but there appears to have been some crossed wires.'

She didn't sound sorry. She sounded snippy and cornered, which pleased him almost as much as the pulse jumping in the base of her throat.

'Then let me uncross them for you,' he said calmly, dropping down onto one of the sofas and stretching out his long legs just as if this were his sitting room and he had returned from a day at the office. 'You and I are getting married. As you know, it's a matter of some urgency so it will be a short engagement.'

'It will not be a short engagement,' she snapped.

'You want to marry me now?' He feigned surprise purely for the purpose of watching her cheeks flush with colour. 'I mean, today would be a difficult ask, but if we leave now, we could be in Vegas by sunrise—'

'I'm not going to Vegas to get married. I'm not getting married, full stop.' Her lips parted in a way that made him feel adrift and in those few sharpened seconds, he could have reached out into the space between them and touched her cheek.

'Once was enough.'

She glanced away, the movement making her glorious red hair look molten in the sunlight. But his gaze followed her right hand as she moved to touch the plain gold band on her ring finger and a primitive drum roll of jealousy buzzed across his skin.

Even now, all these years later, he could still remember the shock of reading the news of her engagement. And it had been an entirely justifiable reaction because just one week after she had abruptly ended things with him, she had got engaged to her prince.

It had been more than simply a shock. Way more. Like the ground opening beneath your feet.

Of course, outwardly, he was doing fine. His company, VFA, had gone public on the stock market last year and turned him into the youngest centibillionaire on the planet. Two weeks ago, *Eras* magazine had named him their 'Person of the Year'.

But beneath the surface, he was still scrabbling at the edge of the abyss.

Had she been seeing Alberto at the same time as she was tucking herself in beside him and laying her head on his chest?

It stung to even ask the question. He couldn't contemplate answering it.

What cut the most was that he had been her first. At the time, and against his own will almost, he had liked that fact a little too much. But afterwards, when he'd found out about Alberto, he had felt used. Felt as if she had only got with him so that she could rehearse for the main performance.

He hadn't wanted the man dead, though— not all of the time anyway—and he had been shocked to read about the accident.

And clearly Betty still felt that shock. That loss.

Abruptly he got to his feet.

'Unfortunately, on this occasion, that decision

is not up to you. I know this must be hard for you, Princess, but sometimes in life we have to make compromises.'

'But you can't want this, Vero?'

His name in her mouth knocked the breath out of his chest. Living in the US, he had got used to people pronouncing his name wrong. All their history seemed to be wrapped in those two short syllables.

It made his brain feel grazed.

She hesitated and he heard her try to swallow as if there was something in her slender throat. 'You don't want this. You don't want me. And I certainly don't want you.'

The sunlight was still streaming in through the window, bright and joyfully oblivious of the tension in the room and in the spine of the slim, red-haired woman standing statue-still on the antique rug. Because she was tense, and not just because she wanted him gone.

But because she was lying.

Betty had always wanted him. Out of all the lies and half-truths she had told him and the secrets he had kept from her, that was the one truth that had stayed true and inviolable, truer and more unassailable than any marriage vow.

She hadn't loved him or needed him or re-spected him, but she had desired him, and with an intensity that had knocked him sideways. It was the reason why he hadn't noticed all the warning signs, that wanting. It had felt so good. Put simply, he'd been flattered, and enough to confuse lust with love.

He wasn't confused now.

Hadn't been confused with any woman since. He wasn't cruel or manipulative, just pragmatic and straight to the point. And thanks to the algorithms of dating apps, it was easy to get straight to the point.

The *sine non qua* of dating was to know what you wanted. Did you want a relationship, or did you just want to meet someone new and have some fun? And by fun, he meant sex.

The simple, no-strings kind. One night or late afternoon or even early morning of pleasure in some anonymous but comfortable hotel. And afterwards, he might hang around long enough to bolt down a cup of coffee and a bagel. No, actually, he had never done that. Prolonged proximity led to intimacy and intimacy tended to negate casualness.

But it was a possibility. Anything was a possibility.

Except falling asleep with someone. That he couldn't do. Sleep was when you were at your most vulnerable. It required a level of trust he simply didn't have, had never had. The only exception was Betty.

She was the one woman he had opened up to. Within reason. Thankfully, he had never told her he loved her.

But he had shared his hopes and dreams and his need for her. That had spilled out during sex when her arms would tighten around him, and her face would go soft and urgent, and he would hear himself babbling a garbled stream of all the things he wanted to do to her and where he needed her to touch him and how beautiful she was.

And again and again, over and over, how much he wanted her.

He still wanted her now, and he knew that there must be something deeply wrong with him for feeling that way. But if there was, then there was something wrong with her too, because whatever she was saying about not wanting him, her body was saying the opposite. Shouting it, in fact, he thought, his eyes grazing her flushed cheekbones and the taut flex of her spine and that slight quiver across her skin as if she was having to hold something in.

She was.

He knew, because he was holding it in too.

'Is that what you told him? Your prince?'

He took a step towards her. 'Did you lie to him like you lied to me?' She blinked—or was it a flinch? But there was no time for him to answer that question because now she was walking towards him, her grey eyes churning and turbulent like a sky filled with nimbostratus clouds.

'You are the liar.' Her voice was shaking now, and, despite himself, he wished it were her body shuddering beneath his. 'And you know nothing about A-Alberto.' She stumbled over the name, emotion resonating in her voice, and now he wished he'd never mentioned the other man. 'You know nothing about him or our relationship. Or me.'

He held her gaze, suddenly furious at having introduced her husband into the conversation. 'Oh, I do know you, Princess Bettina. I was your first—'

'But not my last—'

'Wrong,' he said then, his heart hammering in his chest. 'Your father wants an heir; your family needs one. A legitimate one,' he added, and it cost him to say those words. 'Which will mean having sex with your husband. Me.'

She stepped forward, her hands trembling by her sides and then she was pushing them against his chest.

'I don't want to have sex with you.' Her voice was barely audible as her fingers curled into the lapels of his jacket and, of its own volition, his hand rose to her waist.

'I don't want to have sex with you either,' he said hoarsely, because they were both lying now. And because in the same way that two negatives made a positive, two lies made a truth.

And this, this blistering, gravitational energy between them, was as true now as it had been nine years ago.

For a few seconds, nothing happened and then she was pulling him towards her, closing the distance between them and her mouth was on his—

Her scent enveloped him, and she was leaning into him and in the pull of her desire he felt both peace and pandemonium. And hunger…

A hunger like he had never known.

He could feel it pounding in his veins as his hand splayed against her back and in her openmouthed kiss. As she licked into his mouth, he lost himself in the taste of her desire and the eager, straining press of her body and the feel of her fingers scrabbling at his shirt. The room was blurring and spinning around them just as if they were in the eye of a storm and he felt dizzy and intoxicated, hurtling towards a pleasure that knew no equal.

With a moan, Betty jerked free of his grip and pushed him away so fast and so urgently that he felt dizzy for a different reason.

'No—' She was stumbling backwards, her irises trembling like a millpond in the rain. Her face looked small and stunned. 'No, I don't want this.'

Didn't want it? The lie grated against his ears. He stared at her, his head spinning. Even now, when he knew who she was, she was still playing games.

He glanced down pointedly at his dishevelled shirt.

'You think?'

'I hate you.'

'I don't care,' he said, and that she was still lying to him, to herself, made his voice rough then, brutal even. 'And I don't care that you don't want to marry me. Because, Princess Bettina, in four weeks' time, you and I are going to be married whether you like it or not.' He stared down steadily into her huge, dazed eyes. 'You know, your father offered me a plot of land out in the hills as part of your dowry, but I'm happy to take that kiss as a down payment.'

She sucked in a breath.

'Get out—'

Her face was flushed with an anger that should have made her look ugly but instead highlighted the luminosity of her skin.

'Don't worry, I'm going.' Without bothering to straighten his shirt, he strolled towards the door. He stopped beside it, his hand resting lightly on the handle, and turned to face her. 'But I believe your father has arranged a dinner to celebrate our engagement, so we'll meet again tomorrow evening, Your Royal Highness. You can be sure of that.'

CHAPTER THREE

BETTY WATCHED THE door close, her breath churning in her chest. The normal steady lub-dub of her heart sounded like a runaway train.

I don't want this.

I don't want this.

Her words echoed inside her head, scraping up scornfully against the tingle of her lips from when she had pressed them against Vero's.

She had pressed her lips against his.

She moaned softly. How had that happened? Like some director of a stage play, she blocked their movements around the room, trying to work out how she and Vero had ended up being close enough for that kiss to happen. It wasn't that hard to do. But it didn't answer the question that needed answering, which was what was wrong with her?

As she remembered how she had leaned in to kiss him, her hands curled into fists. It was bad enough that somewhere inside that beautifully shaped skull of his, he had a detailed memory bank of all her sexual preferences plus a few audio files too, of the noises she'd made. But that had been then, back before she knew the truth about him and his motives.

Back before she knew what lay beneath that curling smile and drowning green gaze.

But she knew now, had known for nine years that Vero Farnese had wanted her for one thing and one thing only.

Her title.

The worst part was that even before her mother had warned her to be on her guard with Vero, she had known that her judgement was flawed. Known it, lived it, and finally learned from it.

But she had wanted him so badly.

She had tried to hold back, to remember who she was and what she was supposed to want and who she needed to be with for the future of Malaspina, but it had burst out of her, the words exploding like pollen from a pine tree in spring. And after she'd told him that she wanted to be more than friends, his face had grown taut and her pulse had gathered inside her, dancing and leaping and staggering as he'd leaned in and kissed her.

She had been so in love. Vero had filled her thoughts awake and asleep and she had wanted him to be her first, her only. She knew now that he hadn't loved her, but he hadn't been going to turn her down out of some heightened sense of honour. Mainly because he didn't have an honourable bone in his body.

Any more than she appeared to have a sense of self-preservation.

Her eyes jerked down and she stared at her bag as if it had suddenly turned into a snake. Her phone was ringing.

Was that him? She didn't want to speak to Vero, not now, not ever. She reached for her bag, breathing out shakily as she saw the name on the screen.

It was Bella.

'Sorry, I forgot you were summoned.' Her sister lowered her voice. 'Are you still with Papà?'

Betty closed her eyes. Bella was not a child but nor was she fully adult—emotionally anyway—and that conversation she'd just had with her father was not something she could imagine sharing with her sister. Nor did she want to. Let Bella stay young and carefree for as long as possible.

It was the least she could do.

'No, he left a little while ago.'

'What did he want?' Her sister hesitated. 'He hasn't changed his mind about me going to Switzerland, has he?'

'No, of course not.' Betty pressed her hand

against the bridge of her nose. It felt as if someone were tightening a vice around her head.

'So, what was it, then? Why did he drag you back?'

'Nothing really. He spoke to Nonno this morning and you know that agitates him.' The truth or a version of it would come out soon enough but she didn't want to risk something slipping out about Vero if she told Bella any more than that. 'Anyway, why are you calling?'

'Because Marcus says he's going to come and visit me in Switzerland. And he thinks he has an idea for getting Balius to stop freaking out over the Liverpools.'

Balius was Bella's favourite horse. She was a talented equestrian and had dreams of competing in international events for Malaspina in the future. Right now, she was taking part in shows mostly in Europe, but Balius was struggling with the water jumps.

'That is good news,' Betty said quickly, grateful for the change of topic.

'And he sent this photo of Nightingale. Isn't she lovely?'

Her phone pinged and she stared down at the photo of a beautiful chestnut mare. Standing beside her was the real reason for Bella's excitement. Marcus was very sweet-looking, and puppyish, very young.

Had she ever been that age? If so, she couldn't remember it.

Truthfully, she felt old. Some days she would look at her reflection and be shocked to see the young woman staring back at her. But then since her mother's death she had been treading water.

No, that was too active, she thought as Bella continued to talk.

For so long now, she had been living like some creature in a tank at the zoo. Without her noticing, her widowhood had gone from weeks to months then years and her routine had barely changed. There had been no dating or even much socialising. Through fear or inertia, she was living vicariously through Bella but, beneath her outward composure, she had been chafing at her life. Wanting to break free. To let go.

Picturing that kiss with Vero, she felt her face heat as if she had dunked it in scalding water. She had certainly got her wish, and in the process she had humiliated herself.

So, was it worth it?

A beat of heat pulsed down her spine and she felt her skin quiver like the ground in the aftermath of an earthquake.

Yes.

No.

Yes.

She licked her lips, remembering the feel of

his mouth on hers and that snap of electricity as if he had woken her not from sleep but from something deeper and darker. He had tasted so good, and his hand around her waist had felt better than good. It had felt right.

Curling her fingers, she let her nails bite into the flesh of her palms, welcoming the distracting sting of a different kind of pain, one that couldn't ravage her heart.

It was too late to change what she had done. She was just going to have to chalk it up to shock and abstinence and put it to the back of her mind.

Right now, she needed to focus on the bigger picture, which was this sham of a marriage that her father and Vero had apparently signed off on without so much as a word of consultation with her, the bride.

Her gaze moved jerkily to the rooftops of Morroello and she breathed in deeply, trying to quieten the scamper of her heart. The idea of fighting both her father and Vero made panic slither up inside her and pound against her from the outside all at once. She wasn't sure she could fight the two of them, but she was going to have to because she was not going to marry Vero Farnese.

So, first things first, who else knew about this aside from her father, Vero and herself?

She bit into her lip. Maybe Anselmo, her father's private secretary. But obviously, his silence was a given. Possibly the bishop, but that would all have taken place behind closed doors. Which meant, currently at least, that details about her upcoming nuptials were contained and therefore still negotiable.

She just needed to talk to her father and persuade him that there was another way.

What it was, she didn't know. But what mattered was nipping any talk about this marriage to Vero in the bud.

Ten minutes later she was heading out of Morroello into the Malaspinian countryside. Switching on the air con, she flicked the indicator and overtook a dark grey saloon, taking pleasure in her car's acceleration and the timing of her gear change. And the resentful, indignant expression on the driver's face.

At least there was one man she could outrun and outwit.

These occasional journeys when she was behind the wheel, testing the limits of the car, timing the gear changes and the judicious application of the brakes, were pockets of freedom in a life that was curtailed by a raft of rules, many of which felt as if they had been drafted in the Middle Ages.

Some probably had.

She had always found the palace protocols exhausting, but since Alberto's death it had got so much worse. Now as well as being exhausted, she felt trapped, suffocated by a widowhood that seemed to cast a shadow that stretched further and wider with every passing day so that both the present and the future were just a dark, shapeless cloud.

Only now that cloud had taken the familiar but unwelcome shape of Vero Farnese.

Her fingers tightened around the wheel. It was so typical of her father to simply disappear off to Arduino. No matter that he had tossed a grenade into her life.

But then Prince Vittorio would argue that it wasn't her life. That, as a princess, she didn't have a life, simply a role.

And there was no point in getting angry about that. No point in listing everything she had been denied. For starters, it would be ridiculous and insulting for a princess to whine about a lack of opportunities.

But it still felt as if she had done nothing except be the latest in a long line of Malaspinian princesses, a position she had achieved solely by virtue of her birth. Her academic prowess was just a memory, untested and unchallenged in the real world and, aside from a few months working in the PR department of her father's favourite charity, she had never had a job.

'You are doing something far more important than any job, Bettina. You are performing your duty.' Her shoulders stiffened automatically as her mother's voice echoed inside her head, quiet and glacially cool.

Her mother, both her parents, had been obsessed with duty, and she understood that, for her, that meant being a princess. Being endlessly composed, smiling serenely at every public appearance, listening intently to diplomats and presidents and other regnal heads of state. That she could do, and did, very successfully. Since her mother's death, she had stepped up to be by her father's side. But away from the cameras and the crowds, it felt as if she was still on duty. Always a princess.

Never just Betty.

Except once.

She felt her stomach twist then rise up towards her throat. Only that had been a lie. In postcard-perfect Malaspina there were so many.

But she wasn't going to be part of another one.

Her father was painting beneath one of the huge oak trees that marked the end of the Castello's formal gardens.

Outside, away from the opulence of the palace, he looked smaller and frailer. But she pushed back against the flutter of tenderness as he turned towards her, his face oddly soft in the late afternoon sunlight.

'Bettina. I didn't realise we had a second appointment today.'

'We didn't. We don't, and I'm sorry to interrupt your downtime, Papà.'

Her father winced. He hated modern slang. Although he was more tolerant when Bella used it.

'I hope it is worth the interruption.'

'It is,' she said quickly. 'I met with Vero. And I know that you want me to marry him and I understand your reasoning, but it's just not a viable option.'

'Viable?' her father repeated. He looked calm and, in the sunlight, his snowy hair looked almost like a halo.

'What happened nine years ago was a whim. A caprice. But we aren't compatible. We never were, and I didn't understand that when you intervened. But you were right, Papà,' she said, hoping that he might be more susceptible to flattery than pleading. 'We can't be in the same room together.'

Picturing that moment when she had pulled Vero closer and kissed him hungrily, she felt her face grow warm.

'I see.' He nodded. 'That is unfortunate and

I did wonder whether you would be able to put your ego behind your duty—'

Her eyes were suddenly stinging. 'That's not fair, Papà.' She was irritated, hurt, frustrated, but her words sounded stupid as soon as they left her mouth. They made her sound like some sulky child.

'Fair.' The softness in his face dissolved. 'Fairness is not a criterion in these matters. I am surprised and somewhat disappointed that I still need to explain that to you. And yet, I am not. You have a persistent ability to disappoint me. But if you will not do it, then I cannot make you.'

Was that it? She stared at him in confusion. She had expected Armageddon, or what amounted to Armageddon in her father's world of protocol and restraint. So, an argument. Some kind of extended lecture at the very least, but he had already turned back to his easel.

'Are you agreeing, then? That I'm not going to marry Vero?' she said slowly. When he nodded, she wanted to feel relief and she did, but there was something odd and slippery about the moment that made her heart flutter.

'I do. But,' her father said quietly, his brush hovering over a smudge of green oil paint, 'the situation hasn't changed. Your grandfather is still having a child and that will have repercussions unless we, as a family, can demonstrate to our people that we are fit for purpose.'

He turned then, his eyes reaching hers, their blue irises cool and pragmatic and not at all panicky. In fact, he seemed preternaturally calm, just as if he had a plan B.

A shiver scampered across her skin as her brain frantically tried to catch up.

'I had assumed, naturally, that as my eldest child you would step forward, for the greater good. But fortunately, I have another daughter. And she has a suitor too. And he is both a wealthy and a titled man.'

She felt the ground tremble beneath her feet or maybe it was she who was trembling. She stared down at her shaking hands.

'No.' She hadn't been able to say the word on her own account, but now it rose from her throat explosively. 'No, Papà, Bella is too young to settle down. She has plans, dreams—'

The Prince raised an eyebrow. 'By your own account, she has grown up a lot in the last year and become much more aware of her role. And is already thinking about the future of Malaspina. Your words, Bettina, not mine.'

So that was why he had asked her all those questions? She felt sick and stupid and suddenly full of a fury that she had never felt before.

'She's planning her birthday party, not her marriage. She's not ready—'

Her father was staring at her, a pitiless expression on his face that made her bite the inside of her cheek.

'She is the same age as you were when you married Alberto.'

'That's not the same.'

'How is it not the same? I had an offer for your hand and you agreed to the marriage, now I have an offer for your sister and she will agree to marry too.'

It wasn't the same because she hadn't cared about her life at that point. She had been so wretched and so uncaring about her happiness because after Vero had broken her heart, she hadn't imagined ever being happy again. Nothing had mattered, including who she married.

But Bella was happy. She had friends, a boy she liked and a placement at a university in Geneva. She was so excited about her new life.

'Then let me marry him.'

Her father was shaking his head. 'He wants your sister.'

'I can change his mind. I'll talk to him—'

'Prince Hans von Marburg has some, shall we say, archaic views of marriage. Unlike Alberto or Signor Farnese, he requires a virgin bride.'

She barely registered the censure in her father's remark. Her lungs felt as though they were full of lead. It was impossible to breathe. Alberto had been a decade older than her, but Prince Hans von Marburg was nearly twice as old as Bella.

'She can't marry him. I won't let that happen.'

Her failure to protect her sister once before had led to Bella being taken to hospital in an ambulance. She could not let her be traded into a loveless marriage of convenience.

But how could she stop it? Bella would cry and plead but she knew that her father would not relent. And so Bella would crumble.

She felt almost drunk with despair. Her mind was racing, looking for exits, for some drop-down ladder that could give her a way out. But there was only one way that this could end.

'Your Royal Highness, has it been hard carrying on a courtship without anyone knowing?'

Betty smiled. 'We're very fortunate to have been able to spend time together out of the public eye.'

She was standing next to Vero in the great entrance hall of the Prince's Palace. Dressed in his ceremonial robes, the Lord Chamberlain had just announced their engagement officially to the assembled media.

Hearing her and Vero's names read out had

made it shockingly, undeniably real. The one consolation was that, as a result of her agreeing to marry, her father had agreed to let Bella have the option of rejecting any suitors.

One of the court reporters from the Italian TV network Canale 20 held up his hand. 'It must have been a huge decision for you to marry again after losing His Royal Highness Prince Alberto,' he said, making a small, deferential bow in her direction. 'What made you so sure that you were ready to wed now?'

She felt her smile stiffen.

Because I had no choice. Because my father, the Prince, was going to marry off my sister to a man old enough to be her father.

For a moment, Betty imagined what would happen if she told the mass of reporters and photographers and camera crews the truth.

But there was no room for the truth in Malaspina.

'I haven't been able to think about anything else,' she said slowly. Which was true. She had thought of nothing else for the last twenty-four hours.

Her fingers moved to touch the diamond and 'pigeon's blood' ruby engagement ring that had replaced the band that Alberto had given her on their wedding day. 'It was instant and overwhelming.' Also true.

'So it was love at first sight?'

Yes, she thought, her throat tightening. Nine years ago it was love and longing and need, a physiological need to see him, touch him, be with him as imperative as air or water or sleep. Although she hadn't slept. She had been unable to miss time awake, time with Vero.

She forced herself to smile.

'Not quite. We knew each other already—'

'Did you feel any pressure to remarry, Your Royal Highness?' An American reporter this time. Female, lush and blonde and wearing a smile that wouldn't look out of place on a crocodile.

Her own smile didn't so much as flicker. 'There's always pressure on an heir to the throne to find a partner. I think probably I felt less than most people my age and, in my position, having already been married. But that's one of the reasons that Vero is going back to the States. He wanted to give me the space to make up my mind—'

It was the first time she had spoken his name out loud in public and as the long e and short o reverberated through her body it felt oddly exposing.

That wasn't true. It was something her father had insisted she say to shut down exactly that kind of probing question, so she should have been relieved. But instead, her stomach clenched at the lie.

'But you said yes straight away.' The blonde reporter was gazing dazedly at Vero as if any other option would be an act of madness. Betty gritted her teeth. Have him, she wanted to snap at the woman. You're welcome to him. He might look like a prince but he has no principles, no conscience and no heart.

A British reporter thrust his microphone upwards. 'The House of Marchetta has always followed tradition in their choice of royal consort. Your engagement to Mr Farnese could be seen as a radical step. Some people are saying it amounts to a revolution in royal terms. What are your thoughts on that, Your Highness?'

She felt Vero's hand tighten a fraction around her waist, drawing her closer, and all those hours spent preparing her response to that exact question had all been for nothing as her brain stumbled. Never mind a royal revolution, Vero had turned her life upside down. He made her unstable, made her question everything, question herself.

Blinking, she met the reporter's gaze. 'It would be a unique revolution indeed if it came from inside the palace.'

There was laughter then and she waited for it to die down. 'My family and I are respectful of tradition, but my father Prince Vittorio's reign has been remarkable not just for its stability but its modernity. My marriage to Vero, a Malaspinian citizen, merely reflects that.'

There was another onslaught of questions.

'It will be a short engagement. Is there any reason for that?' The blonde reporter again.

'Might I answer that?' She felt her spine stiffen as Vero leaned forward and she felt the faint trace of his stubble against her jaw. 'I know it feels like this has all happened overnight but Princess Bettina and I grew up in the palace so we had already got to know each other.'

She felt a flicker of annoyance, and something that even more annoyingly felt like admiration. She had been raised from birth to deal with the press. Even as a shy, self-conscious child, she had been forced not just to attend public engagements but to speak at them.

And yet, out of the two of them, Vero seemed more at ease in front of the cameras than she did. But then the cameras loved him. As did some of the crews, she thought, catching sight of the blonde reporter's rapt face again.

'But you were the son of the chauffeur then.' The American reporter persisted. 'Isn't it a tremendous change to go from playing games with the Princess to marrying her?'

His green eyes rested on Betty's face and she

stared almost hypnotised as he reached out to tuck a stray curl behind her ear.

'Less than you think.'

He closed the distance between them and kissed her on the mouth and for a few drugging seconds the world shrank to the feel of his lips on hers and his hand against her waist, and a pleasure that was both dizzyingly immoderate and yet left her wanting more.

There was a sound like popcorn exploding in a pan as about thirty cameras flashed in unison and she could practically feel the combined happiness and relief of the assembled media who had the picture they'd come for.

'I'm sorry, that's all we have time for.' Anselmo stepped forward smoothly as Vero broke the kiss. 'But thank you very much for joining us today.'

'This way, darling,' Vero murmured, taking her hand and leading her back into the private part of the palace and away from the reporters, who were still shouting out questions.

A sleek, dark unmarked car was waiting for them. As the chauffeur closed the door behind them, she snatched her hand free.

'I really don't see that there's any need for me to come with you to the airport,' she said stiffly as Vero stretched out his long legs and tugged his tie loose. 'It's a private airfield. There won't be any reporters.'

She had thought that first meeting at the palace was awkward and uncomfortable, but the press conference had been a hundred, a thousand, times worse. For the last hour, she had been forced not only to hold Vero's hand but also to look into his eyes as if he alone gave her world meaning, and the whole charade was so frustrating she wanted to snatch the ceremonial staff from the Lord Chamberlain and snap it into splinters.

But, of course, she couldn't do any of those things. Particularly not when there were reporters around.

Gone were the days when the Marchetta family could expect a strict media blackout on sensitive and possibly inflammatory situations. Nowadays news outlets paid lip-readers to scan famous couples' mouths as they chatted in private. They employed experts to 'read' their body language and then made up headlines to suit their interpretations of a glance or a frown.

If only she could just tune Vero out somehow.

But there was something vital and shimmering and intensely physical about his presence. It didn't help that he had a body that was more suited to a professional athlete, a tennis player maybe or a swimmer, rather than the typical slack-faced, slightly out of shape businessmen who made up his peers.

'We are supposed to be madly in love and I am not going to be back in the country for another three weeks so obviously you would want to say goodbye to me.'

Tilting up her chin, she glowered at him. 'If only it were goodbye.'

'Careful, *dolcezza*,' he said softly. His gaze encompassed the chauffeur and the close protection officer sitting in the passenger seat. 'You and your father wouldn't want any rumours about the perfection of our upcoming marriage reaching the media.'

She held his gaze. 'Are you suggesting that a trusted member of my staff would leak our private conversation?'

He didn't quite roll his eyes. Vero had never done that even as a teenager. Unlike most of the boys his age, including the ones with titles, he hadn't hidden his shyness or inexperience with girls by goofing around. On the contrary, there had been something restrained about his responses.

Her pulse dipped like a plane hitting turbulence. Not all his responses, she thought, picturing how he had used to shake when they had been together but not alone. As if having to hold himself back.

She felt her pulse crash-land. Because he had been holding something back. The truth of his motives. He had admitted them and then gone on to speak to her in a way that nobody had ever spoken to her. Not even her father at his worst. There had been a hostility and a savage precision to his words so that afterwards she'd felt as if she'd been filleted, and every blistering syllable had been accompanied by that blistering green gaze.

That gaze zeroed in on her now. Still cold, still green but less withering and more incredulous.

'I thought the palace was a closed world. I didn't realise it was a different planet. Yes, I am suggesting that, for the obvious reason that it's exactly what has been happening. Or are all those stories about Frisky Frederico just figments of some overactive reporter's imagination?'

She hated that.

Watching Betty's face stiffen, Vero felt a nip of satisfaction. She hated not just that there were skeletons in her wardrobe but that they were bursting out through the doors and onto smartphone screens all over the world.

But he had to stop with the point scoring. It was childish and more importantly it was counterproductive. Mostly it left him feeling more

churned up than if he'd left it alone. That was
the best-case scenario.

The worst was something he still regretted
now.

He hadn't gone to confront his birth father
with the intention of letting things get so out of
hand. In the main it had been curiosity but a part
of him had been excited. His father was a duke!
And discovering that Tommasino was not his
'real' father had answered so many of the questions he'd had. But it had thrown up even more.

He had been a typical teenager, spilling over
with hormones and contradictions. He'd wanted
to be heard but left alone. He'd loved his parents but he felt as though they came from another planet. And then he'd found out the truth
by accident.

He'd been curious, nothing more, when he'd
stumbled across his birth certificate. But his curiosity had turned to shock and disbelief when
he'd seen the name of his father. It had taken several minutes for his brain to accept what his eyes
had been seeing. An hour at least before he had
been able to confront his mother, and the man
who both was and wasn't his father.

They had argued. But only when he'd said he
wanted to meet the man who had fathered him,
then given him up. His mother had wept and

pleaded, and he had shouted. Only Tommasino had stayed calm.

He should have listened to them. He should have waited. But he hadn't been willing or capable of waiting.

Had he expected to be welcomed like some prodigal son? No. He wasn't that naive, but he had assumed that the Duke would at least be curious about the son he had never met.

He'd been wrong.

The Duke had been quietly appalled at the sudden appearance of his bastard son, but after the initial shock had worn off it had been clear that he was completely and unapologetically uninterested in forming any kind of bond, and certainly not with some impulsive, scruffy teenager who hadn't even known how to address him correctly. To him, Vero was simply a reminder he didn't want of an affair he'd rather forget.

Feeling the Duke evaluate him and find him unworthy of the complications he would bring to his life had hurt, and he had lashed out because he had been a teenager. His father had not simply disowned him to his face, but revealed that he had paid Tommasino to marry his mother and adopt Vero as his own.

The message was clear: stay away, you're not wanted here.

But he was no longer some powerless teenage

boy. He was a man now, a man who was about to marry a princess. As the Duca d'Arduino, he would be equal to his father, and then, in a year's time, following protocol he would be Prince Vero of Malaspina, and the man who'd had him removed from his home would have to, not just acknowledge him, but bow to him too.

The car was slowing. Ahead of them, his private jet sat on the runway, white and streamlined like a gull at rest.

'You shouldn't believe everything you read in the papers.' Her voice was taut and quivering like an overstrung bow, but he was distracted by the way it made that bee-stung mouth of hers tremble.

'And you shouldn't act the fool. It doesn't suit you.'

Her chin jerked up but he was already reaching her hand and uncurling her fingers, half guiding, half pulling her from the car.

'There might be a privacy screen, but your driver and bodyguard have got eyes and who knows? Either one of them might have a gambling addiction. Or a huge mortgage that they've fallen behind on. Or a grandfather with multiple mistresses who need paying off to keep quiet,' he said as they walked swiftly towards the jet.

Her eyes flashed and he felt her hand tense with frustration. But then it must be hard for a natural-born liar like her to hear the truth spoken out loud.

'That's how it works. One tempting offer and the next thing you know our conversation will be a headline.'

He watched as she shook hands with the air stewards and the pilot and co-pilot, bestowing each of them with one of those smiles that she was so famous for. The smile that was as exquisite as a Golconda Diamond. The kind of smile that was only natural to a princess who'd grown up basking in the love and approval of everyone around her and was certain of her place in the world.

She was still smiling as the crew retreated but her eyes were wary and distant.

'Not everyone is as self-serving as you.'

'Or they don't like to admit it. They like to see themselves as better than other people.'

Her lip curled at one corner.

'Probably because, in your case, they are.'

She tried to pull her fingers free then, but he simply tightened his grip, daring her to make a scene, knowing she wouldn't. That wasn't Her Most Serene Royal Highness Princess Bettina's way. She preferred to dazzle her victim then lead him to the edge of the cliff and shove him off.

He leaned forward, tilting his head to one side so that, to anyone watching, it would look as if he were about to kiss her.

'You know, I think you really believe that crown you wear on state occasions is proof that you exist on some moral high ground. And maybe those sycophantic supplicants that surround you at the palace and your adoring subjects believe that too. But you and I both know that no amount of regalia can change the fact that you are a spoiled, self-serving little snob.'

Harsh, he told himself, watching her eyes widen with shock, but fair. Which was more than she had been to him.

Now he kissed her, although it was less a kiss and more a whisper of contact, enough to breathe in her scent and watch her pupils flare. But not so much that he wouldn't be able to sleep. Because someone had to put an end to his body's incoherent and humbling response to her.

He had to put an end to it, otherwise he would run the risk of letting those thoughts that took over his mind turn him into her eager servant just as they had nine years ago.

That wasn't who he was any more. This time, he was in charge.

'I'll see you at the dress rehearsal,' he murmured and then, before she could respond, he let go of her hand and walked swiftly up the stairs and into the jet.

CHAPTER FOUR

'WOULD YOU MIND tipping your head back a fraction, Your Highness?'

Betty's eyes flickered up to meet those of Daniel, the make-up artist who was staring down at her assessingly. 'I'm going to add in a tiny dab of bronzer just here, and here for a snatched effect,' he murmured. 'Bring out those beautiful cheekbones.'

Smiling minutely, Betty tilted her chin up slightly. Daniel was part of her inner circle. He had been doing her make-up since she was a gauche, self-conscious teenager and had helped her evolve from youthful ingénue to the refined, understated look she preferred.

Now, he took a step backwards and smiled. 'Perfect. Now we can move on to your eyes.'

At her first wedding, she'd had little if any input. Her mother had basically made all the decisions and she hadn't cared enough to get involved. This time, her father had taken on that role, reminding her with the precision of a Swiss clock marking the hour that her people were expecting the perfect princess.

She had agreed to everything.

But she needed to be able to look at her reflection and see something of herself today of all days. So, her hair would be in a slightly undone chignon and although her dress was long sleeved with a high neckline, there was a lace-edged cut-out veiled in tulle on the back. As for her make-up, it was determinedly lo-fi. There would be no contouring or ombre or strobing or draping. Just a fluffy lash, a hint of peach blush on the cheek and a swipe of coral-pink balm on the lip. Oh, and freckles.

Her freckles proudly on display.

'Are we okay for time?'

Unlike other brides, a royal bride was never late. But a part of her, the part not bound by duty and protocol, longed to drag her heels. Or better still to stop time so that the hour of her wedding simply never arrived.

'Yes, Your Highness. We have plenty of time.' Taking a step back, Daniel nodded approvingly. 'Your skin is just gorgeous, by the way.'

Betty smiled back at him and her gaze moved involuntarily to the mirror. Was it gorgeous? She always felt so pale and washed out but today her skin did look luminous.

Hopefully it would be enough to convince the

world that she was marrying Vero for love and not because she had been blackmailed into doing so.

The idea that anyone should suspect made her suddenly feel as though she might throw up.

She'd already imagined it happening so many times. At night she would dream that she was standing at the altar and the bishop would ask if there was any known impediment to the marriage taking place and each night a different faceless member of the congregation had got to their feet and she would wake in darkness, her body shaking with panic.

It would be fine, she told herself firmly. Judging by the cards and gifts that had been delivered to the palace, the population of Malaspina were united in their joy and the media outlets were similarly enthused by the prospect of a royal wedding.

Of course, it helped that Vero was one of their own.

Her pulse twitched. And that he looked the part.

Of their own accord, her eyes darted to the magazine lying open on the bed. It was one of the special supplements that had been produced for the wedding. Bella seemed to have all of them so they were all over the palace and every single one had the same photo from the engagement announcement on the front cover.

That kiss.

It had been over in the time it took to press a shutter button. Over before it had started and yet even now just thinking about it, she felt singed inside. And it felt wrong that Vero could make her feel like that. He had lied to her. Led her on. Taken her love and made it feel cheap and ridiculous.

So why did she still get lost in the press of his mouth against hers? It was like being an alcoholic. It didn't matter that she hadn't touched a drop in nine years, one sip, or, in Vero's case, one kiss, was all it took to make her spiral out of control.

'I have something for you.'

Betty glanced away from the mirror to where her sister was leaning forward, her blue eyes shining with excitement.

'Close your eyes. She can, can't she?' Bella looked up at Daniel's assistant, who had been applying tiny individual lashes to Betty's natural ones.

'Of course, Your Highness.'

Smiling at her sister, Betty closed her eyes.

'Okay, you can open them.'

As Betty stared down at the earrings in her hand, Bella leaned forward. 'I know Papà has given you the Valletti necklace and Vero will probably have something special for you too, but

I wanted to give you something just from me. Do you remember when I got them?'

'Of course.' She nodded. It had been the first time her sister had competed, and it had taken hours of pleading to get her father to agree. But it had been worth it. Bella had come first and, as well as a trophy, she had won these earrings.

Betty swallowed. Her eyes were burning. 'They're lovely, and it's so sweet of you to give them to me, but they're yours. You won them.'

Her sister frowned. 'Only because you persuaded Papà to let me compete. I was so happy that day. So when you wear them, I want you to remember that. I want you to remember all the things you do for me and for Papà and everyone else, because you never do. You never put yourself first.'

Until that moment, she had held it together, channelling her panic and fear and anger into efficiency, but now she floundered.

A memory of footsteps pounding down corridors and of her mother's tear-streaked face. Up until that moment she had never understood what the phrase wringing one's hands meant. But watching her mother's fingers clench and unclench in trembling spasms, that had changed her for ever. That day, that one, selfish moment when she had put her ego, her vanity, her pathetic need to be liked above everything, including her sister's life, would live with her for ever. Even now, just hearing her own voice telling Bella that she could have cake, made her squirm with shame and remorse.

'It won't be different, will it? You being married, I mean?' Bella's blue eyes were suddenly bright.

She shook her head. 'Nothing is going to change. Now, help me put these earrings on.'

But life with Vero Farnese was going to change everything.

It was twenty-eight days since she had last seen him.

They had spoken on the phone, short formal conversations that had left her feeling weak and unbalanced. And Vero had sent her flowers every day, which she had dutifully distributed to local hospitals. She had acted surprised, but the flowers had been her idea.

What was surprising was that Vero had requested a 'real' royal wedding. Given that, for her, this was her second marriage and, for both of them, it was purely a marriage of convenience, she had expected Vero to want something small, private, perfunctory.

Only it turned out that wasn't what he wanted. In fact, almost everything he wanted was the opposite of what she'd expected.

But should she be surprised? Vero had always

defied classification. He had grown up in the grounds of a palace but was the son of the chauffeur. His dark hair might be classically Italian but there were those outlier green eyes.

So the wedding venue was not the Lady Chapel at the Palazzo Vanvitelli, the smaller palace used by her grandmother up until her death, but the cathedral. And instead of a minimalist guest list, more than a thousand dignitaries, royals and celebrities would be filling the pews of the Basilica di San Paolo.

She got the feeling from her father's tight-lipped expression whenever the list was discussed that last part hadn't been a request. She didn't know how to feel about that. A part of her would have liked to have witnessed that showdown, but mostly it made her feel nervous.

Even more nervous, because it wasn't as if she'd been feeling relaxed about her upcoming wedding day.

Or the wedding night?

She shivered inside. That too, but that was just part of the general panicky swell that rose up and threatened to swamp her whenever she thought about the post-wedding period of her life. Unlike everyone else, aside from her father and Vero, she was under no illusions that there would be any kind of 'happy ever' attached to their after. Truthfully, she hadn't quite worked out what their version of 'after' would look like. Obviously, it would involve children, an heir and a spare.

First, though, she had to get pregnant.

'Betty? Is everything okay?'

Her sister's voice cut across her train of thought and she reached out and took Bella's hand.

'Everything's fine. And you don't need to worry. I'll always be your big sister.'

And big sisters looked after little sisters even if that meant dancing with the devil. A green-eyed devil without scruples or a heart.

Better that than sacrifice Bella to a loveless marriage with a man twice her age.

Because it was too late for Betty. She had loved and lost, although you couldn't lose what you never had in the first place, could you? And Vero had never loved her.

But then she didn't deserve to be loved anyway because Bella was wrong. She had put herself first and, on each occasion, she had ended up hurting her family.

Selfishly, brutally, stupidly, that one time when she should have looked after her little sister, she had been more interested in looking cool in front of her friends and a boy who had fled from the room when Bella had started to clutch at her throat. But being the focus of positive attention had been such a novelty and so exhilarating that she would have done anything for it not to end. And everyone always preferred Bella. Since her sister's birth, that had been drummed into her and so she had needed her sister to leave. Which was why, despite knowing that Bella's allergies were dangerous, she had let her sister eat the cake.

And then there was Vero. She had wanted him blindly and without thought for the consequences or his motivation in pursuing her. Flattered by his focus, she had let her ego and libido stifle her mother's warnings.

Maybe if she had listened then her mother would never have had that first stroke and then the others wouldn't have followed.

Her fingers tightened around her sister's as the bells of the cathedral rang out the hour. It was time to change into her dress.

Twenty minutes later, Elsa Venturini, the woman who had designed the wedding dress, straightened up from where she had been flicking the fabric of Betty's skirt.

'Would you like to see yourself, Your Royal Highness?' she said quietly.

Betty nodded. 'Yes, but does it—? Do I—?'

'Yes.'

Everyone spoke at once and Bella pressed her

hand against her mouth. 'Oh, Bibi, you look so beautiful. Just like a princess should.'

Betty turned slowly towards the mirror and stared at her reflection, her pulse beating erratically. The dress was undeniably lovely. A simple column of pure white satin with a lace-edged cut-out on the back accompanied by a cathedral-length veil but, even without it covering her face, the woman in the mirror didn't look like her and yet she wasn't a stranger either. She was an idealised version of herself.

The perfect, Most Serene Royal Highness Princess Bettina.

And that was who everyone wanted her to be today.

Particularly the groom.

The carriage to the church was Vero's one concession to her father. The streets were crammed with people craning over the barriers, peering over the heads of the uniformed guards of the Palace, to catch a glimpse of their monarch and their princess. There were Malaspinian flags everywhere and she focused on the fluttering pennants as she waved.

Beside her, her father seemed calm. Thanks to her mother's strictly reinforced mantras about the need never to reveal her emotion, she knew that she looked calm too. But as the Prince helped her out of the carriage, she felt anything but serene.

Run.

The word reverberated inside her like a drum roll or an alarm bell. And in her mind's eye she could see herself picking up the skirt of her dress, then kicking off her shoes and running, head down, like a sprinter.

But then her father held out his arm and she slipped her hand underneath and they climbed the steps to the cathedral.

'Ready?'

No, she thought. Not that it mattered. The Prince's question was rhetorical. There would be no backing down.

She met his eyes and nodded, trying to ignore the feelings of inevitability closing around her like high-sided walls.

As they stepped through the arched doorway into the nave, her heart was lurching against her ribs so heavily that when the guests turned towards her for a moment, she thought it was because they could hear it beating. But, of course, they just wanted to see what she was wearing.

Some of the faces would be familiar. But today they were just blurred ovals. She felt a rush of panic, and then her eyes fixed on Bella's small, heart-shaped face and she remembered why she was there, and that sense of purpose calmed her. Now she could see people. A prime minister here. An actor there. Several footballers and their gazelle-like wives. Some distant relations, the older ones dripping with jewels, their younger counterparts taking furtive glances at their phones, and, dotted in between, a few business colleagues of Vero.

Conspicuous by his absence was her grandfather. Behind the scenes, there had been a standoff with Vittorio refusing to allow Frederico to bring his young bride, but then Nonno had tripped and fractured his ankle and, horrified at the idea of being photographed in a wheelchair, he had decided not to attend on the grounds of mobility.

Also absent was anyone from Vero's family.

He had no siblings; his mother had died the year before and his father was too ill to travel. That fact had emerged at the engagement dinner. Vero had offered no further information and when she had started to suggest that they wait for Tommasino to recover, he had shut her down. He hadn't raised his voice. It had stayed low and cool but he had changed the subject shortly afterwards.

'Smile, Bettina,' her father murmured softly but his eyes were sharp. 'Our people want to see you smile.'

He was right. Former royal brides like her mother and grandmother had been instructed to look serious on their wedding day. Royal weddings were not like ordinary weddings. The bride was not simply taking a husband, often she was forming an alliance. In other words, they had been doing their duty and smiling had therefore been inappropriate.

But times had changed, and today the crowds who came to cheer the bride and groom wanted to believe in the magic, to believe in the happy ever after.

Which meant she needed to smile, but her mouth wouldn't make the right shape. It was as if all the energy in her body were being diverted into her legs, forcing her on to where the tall dark-haired man was standing by the altar.

Alberto had not bothered to turn round. But as she got closer, Vero turned, and she felt her legs waver beneath her and static filled her head and as the green of his irises met her gaze, she had to stop herself from looking away.

Because that was what hurt the most. To have to look into his eyes and not see them soften. Which was beyond stupid given that she knew now that he had been simply playing the part of a man in love. Playing her, so that for a few sweet months she had believed that there might be another way for her to live.

Her throat clenched around the lump forming there.

Growing up, she had never been one of those little girls who fantasised about her wedding day. But nine years ago, she had dreamed about this moment, and with the light slicing through the stained-glass windows she let herself slide back into the time before everything changed when she still believed that Vero loved her for herself. Believed that their wedding would be the day when the whole world would bear witness to their love.

She had let him inside her head and under her skin. Let him get closer than anyone ever had, before or since, even Bella. And she had so wanted it to be real that she had ignored the glaringly obvious truth. That, like so many other poor little rich girls, it was her money and wealth and, in her case, the glitter of her crown, that were the real draw.

It was almost unbearable to compare the naivety of her hopes with the reality of this charade.

And it was a charade, she thought as his green eyes fixed on her face, his features moulded into one of those classification-defying expressions that had fascinated her once but now made her want to weep or rage.

He was astonishingly, unreasonably beautiful. Every woman's fantasy of a bridegroom.

It wasn't just his height or that lean, muscular body or even that absurdly beautiful, sculpted face. He had a kind of gravitational pull that was based on something less tangible than limbs and muscles and bone structure. Not power or wealth. He'd had neither when they'd first met but he'd still had it then. A magnetism that was outside science and science fiction. Nameless. Captivating.

Dangerous.

Prince Vittorio released her hand and stepped back to take his seat and suddenly it was just her and Vero. Alone. In a cathedral filled with over a thousand guests and choristers and musicians and members of the Malaspinian armed forces.

It hurt to look at him, to imagine what might have been, only she couldn't let him know that was what she was thinking and so she trained her gaze on his face.

The service went like clockwork in that it was smooth flowing and, unlike her first wedding, she managed to say her vows without so much as a stammer even though her throat was alarmingly dry.

Marrying Alberto, she had been in a daze, as if she were sleepwalking.

With Vero, everything felt crisp and sharp-edged. The vows slipped from her tongue like rubies and pearls in that Russian fairy tale Bella loved so much, even though they should have been serpents because every word was a lie.

There was only one moment off-script.

When he slid the ring onto her finger, her hand twitched and his eyes snapped to hers and there was something in how he stared down at her that made her feel as if she were a kite caught in a gust of wind, dragged upwards, soaring higher and higher.

Exactly sixty-two minutes later she was walking back out of the church, her fingers no longer resting on her father's arm but interlinked with Vero's as if he were leading her onto a dance floor, his grip both possessive and suggestive. And much as she wanted to, she could think of no way to extricate her hand without drawing attention to it. Of course she had to hold his hand, he was her husband.

Her legs did that wavering thing again. She felt dizzy and precarious, as if she were standing on a windowsill.

For so long there had been a place inside her, a gap, an emptiness, a Vero-shaped hole in her life, and now he was here, and not just here. He was her husband.

'Aren't you forgetting something?'

They had paused at the top of the steps to the cheers of the crowd, and her smile froze to her face, the train of her thoughts cut in two by his quiet but authoritative voice. He was smiling too and even though she knew he was faking it she felt as if every cell in her body were turning towards him and opening like sunflowers at dawn.

'I don't think so.' Mentally, she ticked off all the bullet points in the day's schedule.

'That ceremony was for the bishop and your father. For your people, the fairy tale starts now.'

'Starts how?'

For a moment, he didn't reply. He just stared at her, his green gaze flickering over her face too fast to read the emotion, but she felt every flicker of his eyes stir something inside her and she wanted to look away but he kept looking at her, just looking and looking and all the time there was that hungry undercurrent of restlessness and restraint.

'With a kiss.' And then he leaned in, his irises a deep, drowning green, and fitted his mouth to hers.

It wasn't like that kiss at the palace. That had been an almost involuntary eruption of hunger, a blistering loss of control. This was all about control. *His.* He was kissing her to make a point, to show the world that they were man and wife.

Her man. His wife.

She jerked her head back and he stared down at her, his mouth curving at the corners as he led her down the steps to the carriage as the sound of the crowd's cheers engulfed them.

'You look beautiful.'

It took her a moment to register the compliment because none of the warm afternoon sunlight was threaded through his voice. Instead, it sounded cool with an undertone of something like anger. As if he regretted having spoken. He certainly didn't sound happy about it.

'It's a beautiful dress.'

His pupils flared. 'Yes, it is. But I'm not talking about the dress.' She felt his fingers loosen almost as if he was going to let go of her hand and then, abruptly, they tightened, and she heard his breath catch.

'I'm talking about you. You're beautiful.'

It sounded even less like a compliment and more like an accusation.

'You don't need to tell me that. We're married now so there's no reason to lie. Or rather, there's no reason to add to all the lies we're already telling today.'

His face didn't change but she felt the flex of his muscles as he helped her into the carriage. After the scale of the cathedral, the interior of the carriage felt tiny and Vero seemed to fill it, taking up both space and air as the door closed behind him so that all her senses felt crowded.

As it started to move, he shifted back against the velvet cushions. He looked relaxed but, like a jaguar dozing in a tree, she knew that he wasn't.

'You seem confused, *dolcezza*,' he said slowly.

'That was a real wedding. We made vows in front of a whole cathedral full of witnesses. It's legal and binding, and I meant every word I said. But then I suppose I shouldn't be surprised that you didn't. I mean, you've spent most of your life tossing out lies like some tourist throwing loose change into the Trevi Fountain. Why should your subjects be treated any differently?'

'I don't lie to my subjects.'

'Right, so all those people waving their little flags know that your grandfather has been skimming money from the Marchetta bank accounts to fund his lifestyle?'

She hated him then for being right, for being there in the carriage and for having this power over her. For being willing to wield that power and for that hot, hard light in his eyes.

'And they won't ever know now, will they?' he said softly. 'Thanks to me.'

'Don't make out you're some kind of hero,' she snapped. 'You're getting something out of this too.'

'And you hate that. Hate that my money puts us on an equal footing.'

'You wish.'

He held her eyes for a beat, his mouth a hard line, then he turned towards the window, and as he waved at the crowd, she heard the cheers magnify.

'What a pity that you didn't have a better offer. Another prince waiting in the wings for you.'

'He wasn't waiting in the wings.'

His words stung, again stupidly because he was the bad guy here. He had lied and manipulated her and yet even at the time getting engaged to Alberto had felt wrong for reasons she could neither name nor articulate.

But she hadn't had the energy to argue with her father, not after Vero's deception and her mother's stroke, and so she had agreed to the engagement.

He shrugged. 'If you say so.'

Smarmy bastard, she thought, and his head snapped towards her as if she had spoken aloud.

'I do say so,' she said, her fingers tightening around her bouquet. 'Not that you care what I say or think or feel. You've made that perfectly clear already.'

'Well, opposites attract and let's face it, Princess, nobody could accuse you of being transparent.' He shook his head. 'Your whole life is a performance. Nothing about it is real. Everything is edited and managed and polished to such a shine that everyone is dazzled, but the heart of it is hollow and empty of anything profound or true.'

Her heart stumbled then beat loudly in her chest. Only one person had ever spoken to her like this. The same person who was speaking to her now.

'Then you should fit right in,' she spat at him, goaded now but instantly regretting her words because they made her sound weak and wounded and she couldn't bear for him to know how badly he had hurt her. How much it was hurting to have to be here with him now.

Except he didn't, Vero thought later as he sat at the wedding breakfast, surrounded by a thousand strangers and beside a woman who despised him. He didn't fit here in this world.

That fact had been made painfully clear to him when he was fifteen years old. He might share his father's blood, but he would never be in his life. He was an embarrassment, something to be swept aside, denied, disowned.

But not today.

His eyes narrowed over the assembled guests to the iron-grey head at the far end of the ballroom. In an ideal world, Tommasino and Vero's mother would be here with him on the top table and he hated that they couldn't be.

Either way, having the Duke there was non-negotiable.

That was his revenge. Forcing his birth father to witness the son he had abandoned marrying a princess and publicly having to acknowledge that shift in status. That was why he had demanded a wedding of this scale and why his birth father was currently sitting at the outer edge of the room furthest away from the guests of honour.

The wedding breakfast was being served in the great ballroom, the world-famous Stanza delle Luci. Like most of the guests, he found himself admiring the delicate, embellished plasterwork on the ceiling, the colossal, mirrored doors and the thirty legendary, glittering chandeliers.

Unlike most of the guests, he had seen it before, nearly a decade earlier. He and Betty had misjudged the time one day and the only way for him to get back to meet his father had been to go via the palace. Betty had distracted the footmen so that he could sneak in through a side door.

His body tensed as he remembered the flush of colour in her cheeks. The way her eyes had been wide with panic and excitement and the tight grip of her fingers. Ducking into doorways and under staircases as she'd led him from room to room.

She had pulled him through another door into the ballroom and they had both stopped and stared up at the towering ceiling, and then she had suddenly started to spin on the spot, her head thrown back, her arms outstretched.

Watching her spin, he didn't think he had seen anything so beautiful.

They had spent so much time together, leaning over the engines of various cars, her beautiful clothes covered up by his overalls. And he'd kept telling himself it was all in his head. Those looks. That way her eyes would move shyly but frequently to meet his. All those times they would finish each other's sentences.

But then she had stumbled, and he had stepped forward and steadied her and suddenly she had been in his arms, and she'd been kissing him, and he had realised that all that stuff he'd been thinking was in her head too.

And then he had been spinning as well, and he could taste her panic and her excitement and something that he'd thought was love.

Did she remember that day?

He glanced over at the woman sitting beside him, her head tilted to catch something the bishop was saying.

Perhaps. But not in the way he did. Perhaps not at all. And he wanted to reach over in front of all these strangers and pull her against him and take that voluptuous bow of a mouth of hers and keep on taking until she relinquished herself to her need for him. The need that made them equal.

The breakfast seemed to last an eternity.

There were five courses then toasts, speeches and now it was time for the first dance between the Prince and his daughter.

A hush had fallen on the ballroom and then the musicians began to play a beautiful waltz.

He watched, his blood pounding in his skull as her father spun Betty in a circle, his patrician features breaking into a smile as the crowd broke into polite applause. It had been hard enough sitting so close to Betty and feeling the distance between them. But now it felt as if he were watching her through glass, almost as if she were inside a snow globe, and her beauty and remoteness were a punch to his stomach, a reminder that he was still an outsider, an intruder to be removed.

He didn't realise he was moving until he stopped in front of the Prince. 'Excuse me, Your Royal Highness.' He bowed minutely. 'May I cut in? I'd like to dance with my wife.'

He could tell from the way the Prince's eyes bulged slightly that he had broken with protocol, but he didn't care.

Betty's eyes widened as he held out his hand, but she took it calmly.

There was a smattering of applause as he pulled her closer and now, as if some invisible signal had happened, other couples joined them on the dance floor.

'What are you doing?' she murmured against his cheek.

'Dancing with my wife.'

The chandeliers in the vast ballroom might be the most photographed in the world but nothing could compete with Betty. She looked luminous in that beautiful shimmering dress, pure and remote like a bride in a storybook, but he felt her hand twitch against his as his fingers splayed against her back, and he was suddenly grateful for the lack of direct skin-to-skin contact.

His palm flexed against her back. She felt temptingly good, warm and soft where he was hard, and he had forgotten how good she smelled. Enticingly good, to the point that he couldn't stop himself from leaning and breathing in the scent of her perfume and, beneath that, her skin.

'Scusi...'

Still lost in her scent, he barely glanced up as one of the spinning couples encroached on their space.

The woman bobbed a curtsey, and the man bowed. 'My apologies, Your Royal Highness—'

Vero felt his breath turn to air. He'd played this moment inside his head so many times and in every variation he had been ready for his father, ready to meet his gaze and watch his discomfort, to savour the disorientation. But now, as the Duke glanced past his shoulder, purposely avoiding acknowledging him in any way, he was the one feeling disorientated, dizzy, ripped open.

Ashamed.

And he hated that feeling. Hated that, despite his knowing everything the Duke had done to deny his existence and conceal the connection between them, it was still there inside him. That longing for acceptance.

It was a few seconds at most and then they were moving again, turning in slow circles, Vero's feet moving automatically. He could feel Betty's eyes on his face, and not just her eyes. It felt as if the eyes of everyone in the room were looking at him, as if everything, the tables, the chandeliers, the floral arrangements, were watching him, judging him—

Abruptly, he pulled away. 'I think that's enough dancing for one night.' Ignoring Betty's confusion, he tightened his grip on her hand. 'It's time to leave.'

CHAPTER FIVE

THE DRIVE TO the Marchetta royal residence in Milan took less than thirty minutes. But for Vero it felt as endless as the walk back to a locker room after losing the match.

The housekeeper was waiting for them in the entrance hall and, in an ideal world, the one he had pictured at this point in time, her bobbing curtsey and effusive congratulations would have chimed with his private, triumphant celebrations at having finally got his revenge.

But he didn't feel like performing a victory lap. Why would he?

He thought back to the moment in the ball-room when the Duke cut him. The floor had felt as if it were made of glass. Or quicksand. He had felt like an imposter, an intruder. As if everyone were looking at him and he'd felt their attention as a thief would feel a security spotlight.

Maybe because she hadn't enjoyed being dragged away from her wedding party, Betty had given him the cold shoulder in the limousine, but now she stepped forward, smiling warmly, and, watching her mouth curve upwards, Vero felt a nip of something that was almost like jealousy.

'Thank you, Elena. And thank you for your beautiful gift. I—we love it, don't we, Vero?'

He nodded, noting the correction. Was it normal for a bride to forget she was married on her wedding day? '*We* do,' he said, although, truthfully, he hadn't paid that much attention to the gifts they'd received.

As was usual among engaged royal couples, they had sent their guests a list of charities they wished to support and encouraged them to donate. But there were exceptions. Members of the household staff like Elena, and close friends and family, were permitted to give presents.

But he was only really interested in what Prince Vittorio had given him. Or, more accurately, bestowed upon him. As Betty's husband, he was now to be known as the Duca d'Arduino. And when she took the throne, he would be His Royal Highness Prince Vero.

It had been agreed as part of the wedding negotiations. His marriage to Betty would provide heirs for the House of Marchetta and in exchange he would have a title, one that equalled and would ultimately rank higher than the Duke's.

It was what he had been working towards for years.

At first, it wasn't a conscious ambition, just a vague, nameless need to show the people who had looked down on him and tossed him aside as if he were a scratch card without a prize that they had been wrong.

He wasn't worthless or inferior or disposable. He couldn't be discarded and ignored any more. And he would not prove it in some equally vague, nameless way. He wanted to rub their faces in it.

Meeting Frederico by chance in Cairo had crystallised those shapeless thoughts into a plan. And the plan had worked. Except it hadn't. He had been visible yet unacknowledged.

As if to prove that point, Elena stepped forward to address Betty, ignoring him completely.

'Would you like any refreshments, Your Royal Highness?'

Vero felt a sudden, strong urge for a glass of whisky. Or better still a bottle, although that probably wasn't the best idea. Undoubtedly their early exit from the celebrations would be greeted with approval, but the groom necking a bottle of spirits on his wedding night didn't have quite the same optics.

Betty was midway through shaking her head, and then she glanced over at him, and he knew that she had forgotten that 'you' was now plural.

He felt his throat tighten with the old anger, the anger that he'd worked so hard to contain.

'No, thank you, Elena. I think we might go up.'

The Marchetta residence was modest in comparison to the Prince's Palace. It was only the royal coat of arms with its crown and sceptre and pelican with outstretched wings on the external gates that gave any indication it was a royal residence. Its location in Milan had been another strategic decision, this time by the tenth Prince of Malaspina, to demonstrate the country's close links with its neighbour.

And to offer a handy bolt-hole in case of any revolution, although that was not widely publicised. There would be worse places to sit out a revolution, he thought, his gaze grazing the opulent red wall coverings and the striking painted ceiling as they made their way upstairs. But then his eyes moved of their own accord to the back of Betty's dress.

He licked the back of his teeth.

It had fascinated him all day. The front was modest and high cut but turn her around and there it was. That cut-out. Just a lace-edged oval. Simple, tasteful. But looking at it made him feel like a voyeur.

Tilting his chin, he inched back his head.

There was no bare flesh on display. Nothing so overt for Princess Bettina on her wedding day. Her pale skin was veiled but again that only served to pique a man's curiosity.

His curiosity, and his alone. Because as far as Betty was concerned, there would be no other men.

As for those buttons. His gaze ticked down her spine. Stopping as they did just above the curve of her buttocks, they seemed designed solely for the purpose of tantalising and distracting.

And, more pragmatically, to make it a Herculean challenge to access the tempting body underneath, he thought sourly as the housekeeper led them through a doorway. Not that those buttons were necessary. On the rare occasions they had been alone today, there had been a cool but tangible forcefield of resentment around Betty that made it clear that any intrusion into her private space would result in ice burn or frostbite.

Vero stared around the huge, beautiful bedroom, his blood thudding jerkily in his veins.

'Is there anything I can do for you, Your Highness?' The housekeeper again.

'No, no, thank you, Elena.' Betty smiled. 'I think we have everything we need.' She was tired, he could hear it in her voice. Tired of posing and pretending to be a happy, blushing bride. And she wanted the housekeeper gone so that she could relax. 'Why don't you go and join your family and watch the fireworks?'

'Yes, why don't you do that, Elena?' He slipped his arm around Betty's waist, shifting his weight so that she had to grab his arm to stop herself overbalancing. 'No need to hang around. We'll be fine on our own, won't we, *cara*?'

He could feel Betty's heart beating against his ribs, but she smiled, and she kept smiling right up until the moment when the door closed behind Elena.

Instantly, she jerked free of his grip and stepped backwards, her grey eyes swirling like storm clouds.

'Do you mind?'

'I don't. And you shouldn't either. If you want this marriage to be in any way believable, you need to get into character. We're newly-weds, remember?'

'And when we're in public, we will act like newly-weds. But right now, we're alone.' Her voice was quiet and calm but that grey glare could have given a tornado-building supercell a run for its money. 'So there's no reason for us to touch one another.'

'How about kissing?' he said softly. 'Is there a reason for that?'

A flush, pale like the underside of a rose petal, seeped along the curve of her cheekbones.

'If you're talking about the kiss on the cathedral steps—'

'I wasn't.' He tilted his head, the better to see

her reaction. 'I was thinking back to how you kissed me that first day at the palace.'

'That was—'

'What?' He held her gaze. 'A mistake? A muscle memory.' He watched her eyes widen. 'Do tell, Princess. I'm longing to hear you tie yourself up in knots trying to explain that away.' Better still, he could tie Betty up in knots. Splay her out on that big bed and take his sweet time licking every inch of her.

'Don't call me that. And I don't need to explain anything,' she said coolly. 'Because it meant nothing. In fact, until you mentioned it, I'd forgotten all about it.'

'Liar.'

She took a step towards him, her hands curling into fists by her sides, her eyes dizzyingly close to his, and he wondered whether it was some twisted cosmic joke that she could stand there and lie so emphatically to his face and yet look so innocent and vulnerable in that dress.

'Only because you made me stand up and lie in front of all those people.'

And nine years ago, she had made a fool of him, so maybe they were all square.

No, he thought, not yet.

'And you did it so beautifully, so convincingly. But then look at all those lies your grandfather told, and all the lies your father told and is undoubtedly still telling to cover up those original lies. It's in your blood, isn't it, Your Royal Highness?'

She glared at him, all storm-cloud eyes and that mouth of hers forming a shape that made hunger spark sharply inside him, and for a moment he wanted to cross the room and press an open-mouthed kiss on her mouth and keep kissing until she had no breath left to fight her need for him.

'Your opinions might carry more weight if they weren't simply some regurgitated nonsense you've read online,' she said crisply, her grey eyes beautiful, bored. 'But as you've never met my grandfather, I'd rather you kept them to yourself.'

He felt a pang almost of sympathy. She had no idea that he had met Frederico or that the old man had encouraged him to pursue Betty. As he watched her throat quiver, it was on the tip of his tongue to tell her the truth. But he wasn't ready to share the contents of that conversation in Cairo just yet.

'The same goes for the rest of you. Keep your hands, your mouth, your everything to yourself—'

'And that's your plan, is it, for how we're going to make this work?'

'At least I have a plan. And there is no we.'

She still sounded bored but there was a hoarseness there too that made his chest pull tight.

'You might want to tell your mouth that,' he said softly, mainly to watch her lips part in outrage. 'It seems to have trouble keeping its distance from my mouth.'

She gifted him one of those glacial stares she seemed to reserve for him alone and stalked across the room to the dressing table.

Staring after her, Vero felt his chest tighten.

Betty was wrong. He did have a plan.

It had felt like fate meeting Prince Frederico at the casino in Cairo. He had been on a business trip in the region and his hosts had suggested a visit to neighbouring Egypt to play roulette. He wasn't a big gambler, but he had hit a jackpot of sorts when he had sat down at the baccarat table and his neighbour had turned out to be Betty's grandfather.

He'd never met the Prince, but he'd heard the rumours and, after two hours listening to the old man talk, he could understand why Frederico was there with him instead of sitting on the Malaspinian throne. He was funny, charming, garrulous and indiscreet. In short, everything that made him great company also made him an unsuitable monarch.

After several more whiskies Frederico's tongue had been well and truly loosened and his blue eyes had misted over as he had let slip that he was having a baby with his new, much younger wife.

By the end of the evening, her grandfather had been rambling and repetitive, his charm diminished by alcohol and age, but two things were clear. The old man had no intention of challenging the line of inheritance, but he knew that the pregnancy would send his pompous, pedantic son into a tailspin.

Vero glanced over at Betty, replaying what happened next.

It had been simple enough to set everything in motion.

He'd encouraged the old prince to call his son once the pregnancy was established and then he'd waited. And that had been the hardest part. Judging how much time to let pass before approaching Vittorio. After that, everything had just fallen into place.

And then it had all fallen apart in the ballroom.

Not that anyone would have realised. Betty wasn't the only one who could present a perfect shopfront to the world.

'If you're going to keep this up, this will be a very long ten days,' he said mildly.

'We might be married, Vero, but that doesn't mean that we can just carry on where we left off.'

He shrugged. 'Why not? It's not that different from before. As I recall we had a "no touching" rule in play nine years ago.'

Her beautiful lips pressed into a thin line but there was a huskiness to her voice that was like a match striking kindling.

'That was different. There was no touching in public. This time, there's going to be no touching in private.'

'That's very confusing. What if I get confused? I'm only the son of a chauffeur.'

She sighed. 'You're not confused, you're contrarian.' Her hair was coming loose from where it knotted into some kind of bun at the base of her neck. If only he could pull out those pins, loosen it some more. He'd never been that attracted to redheads, but as usual Betty was his rule-bending exception.

'Not at all. I'll agree to anything and everything you want, just like I always did. But maybe I need to jog your memory.'

The temperature in the room seemed to shift up several degrees.

'Stop looking at me like that,' she said then.

'Like what?'

He knew how he was looking at her, but he wasn't going to let her get off that easily. He watched her face, saw the sideshow of emotions and felt a pang of disappointment as they were replaced by her go-to expression. That serene mask that covered all eventualities from greeting local dignitaries to opening a sports centre. And giving the brush-off to her ex-lover.

Of course, nine years ago he had viewed that millpond composure differently. Back then, it had fascinated him. That she could be so poised and serene in public and then, once they were alone, she would shed her inhibitions with her clothes, becoming decisive, unbound, going from zero to wanton and slowing, much less stopping, had been a concept, not a possibility.

And he loved that switch flicking. Even just thinking about it now made his brain stumble and his skin twitch.

'It's been a very long day. It's time to go to b-bed.'

Her sentence fizzled out as she stuttered around the word bed, and something swelled low in his throat and his head began flooding with memories of when she had stammered out words on other occasions and for different reasons.

'I agree,' he said slowly.

Her pupils flared then, and her eyes narrowed infinitesimally, and he hated that she could do that. That she could build barriers between them on a dime. But then he was making her angry. Which was a different kind of barrier.

'I'm looking forward to it.' Slipping off his jacket, he tossed it onto a small armchair. Holding her gaze, he tugged his tie loose and then the top button of his shirt.

'I'm glad,' she snapped. 'Your bed is through that door. You have your own room.'

'Separate beds? Separate rooms?' He raised an eyebrow. 'And how exactly are you planning on explaining that to Elena and the rest of the staff?' It might be customary among the upper classes, and particularly royalty, for couples to sleep in separate rooms, but even he knew that didn't apply to the wedding night.

'I'm a princess. I don't explain myself to anyone. And as you very well know, I don't share a bedroom.'

'What, even with your husband?'

'You're not my husband. You're just a man who I've been coerced into marrying.'

That stung, more than he wanted to admit. 'Yes, by your father. Who wants an heir. I'm sorry to burst your bubble, Princess, but this isn't *Dumbo*. A stork isn't going to fly by and drop one at the Prince's Palace in nine months' time.'

He tapped the back of the chair. 'Not even a royal pelican can do that.'

'Enough.' Her voice was high and thin sounding, as if she were facing down a storm, the storm he could see in her eyes.

'Enough of what?'

Her irises were huge and limpid. 'Everything. This. You. Today. Being tugged around on strings like some puppet. And you making out it's all a bit of a joke because you don't care that we've just lied to the whole world. To each other.'

'Betty—'

'Just go, please.'

For a moment he held her gaze and then he took a vacillating step backwards, ducking instinctively as she snatched up a delicate figurine from the dressing table and hurled it across the room.

There was a splintering sound as it hit the wall behind him. 'I said get out.'

'With pleasure,' he said and in that moment he meant it. He spun round and stalked towards the connecting door, his fingers gripping the handle as he yanked it open with unnecessary force.

Later, he would wonder why he turned back to look at her. Was it the need to face her down? To have the final word? If there were any words waiting, he forgot them instantly.

Betty had turned and was fumbling with the buttons at the nape of her neck. They were tiny, the kind fastened with looping elastic.

His hand tightened around the handle, his anger unspooling as he watched her tug ineffectually at the loops. Her head was twisted over her shoulder, and she was glancing at the reflection of her back in the mirror, her fingertips straining for the satin-covered buttons. But even if she managed to undo the ones closest, her arm wasn't going to reach others.

Not my problem, he told himself, watching her struggle. But if someone didn't help her, she was going to have to sleep in that dress.

He swore silently.

'Why don't you call Elena?'

She stiffened, but she didn't look over at him as she replied. 'I can manage.'

She couldn't. That much was obvious, but he knew she wouldn't call her housekeeper. She wouldn't call anyone, and not because it would mean having to explain herself. If anyone found her here alone, fighting to get undressed, no explanation would be required.

And all it would take would be one careless word or casual remark…

He let go of the handle and strode across the room towards her.

'Here. Let me—'

She pushed his hand away. 'I don't need any help, especially not—'

'Mine.' He finished the sentence for her. 'But unless you're going to call someone else, then it's my help you're getting. Otherwise, your maid is going to find you in your wedding dress to-morrow morning, which probably isn't going to scream true love and happy ever after.'

Vero was right, Betty thought. But the idea of him unbuttoning her dress made the air around her snap against her skin like a lightning current striking the ground.

In the past, he had loved to watch her undress and she had loved how he had looked at her, his face stilling, growing blunt with a hunger that had matched hers. A hunger that had enveloped her and left her shaking inside. The first time it had happened had been the most erotic moment in her life and he hadn't even touched her. It was the first time she had felt power of any kind and she had slowed down, taking her time, revelling in her power over him until he had lost patience.

Her skin felt hot and tight as she remembered that moment when his control had snapped and the green of his irises had locked onto hers like a big cat, and then he had reached for her, his hands moving with swift, urgent precision.

She felt tears sting her eyes and it would be so easy to let them fall and ease the frantic, spiky static inside her chest. But if she started crying, she might never stop, and the thought filled her with such panic that she couldn't speak or even shake her head.

'Just let me help, Betty. I'm not going to jump you. I may be a lot of things you don't like but I would never do that,' Vero said then and there was an uneven note to his voice that made her chin jerk up.

'I know.' The chemistry between them had sometimes been wordless but he had always waited for that touch of her hand. 'I know that.'

It was ironic really. Princesses, in Malaspina anyway, were required to look modest on their wedding day. That was why she had worn a dress with long sleeves and such a high neckline. Only it was that very same neckline that made it impossible for her to undo the buttons herself and forced her to seek help to undress.

As if he could sense her softening, Vero took a step closer.

'Then let me help. Please.' There was still tension in his voice but that 'please' grazed her skin. He looked heartbreakingly handsome and her imperfectly repaired heart lurched against her ribs as his complex, compelling features regrouped. Now he gestured towards her dress. 'It'll take a couple of seconds.'

It didn't. The buttons were tiny and the satin covering them made it hard for him to get a purchase. She could feel the intensity of his concentration as his fingers moved over her back and she tried not to let herself drift into his gravitational field. But it was hard when he was so close, and she could feel the brush of his biceps as he wrestled with the buttons.

'How many of these damned things are there?'

'There's one hundred and sixty down the back and twenty-nine on each sleeve. They don't all need to be undone,' she added as he raised an eyebrow.

'I thought car engines were fiddly. This is harder than changing a timing chain.'

'Do you still play around with engines?'

His hand stilled against her back and her eyes moved to his reflected face. 'I wouldn't call it playing and, yes, I do. I have a couple of cars I'm rebuilding at the moment.'

Their eyes locked in the mirror. Was he remembering those afternoons in the cool of the garage? She couldn't answer that question. Instead, she stared up at him and he stared back down at her until she couldn't bear it any longer, and maybe he couldn't either because he suddenly jerked his gaze away as if it hurt to look at her.

'Let me just do a couple more.'

He shifted position and, in the mirror, she watched the bands of muscle across his stomach and shoulders flex against the thin material. It should have reduced the impact, seeing them second-hand, but it made her feel like a voyeur. Except she didn't just want to watch. She wanted to touch, to caress, to trace her fingers over his smooth, contoured skin. She wanted to kiss. To lick.

Her pulse twitched at the thought.

'Try now.'

She tried, pulling the bodice forward, but there was still not enough room. 'One more maybe?' she said, shaking her head.

He undid another button and without warning the dress slipped over her shoulders and she clutched it closer.

'Sorry—' His eyes were very green on hers.

'That's okay. Thank you,' she muttered.

He stared at her in silence, nodded and then took a step backwards.

He was leaving. Her stomach cramped, the tension of the last four weeks, and of the wedding and the guilt of lying to the world and the shame of being powerless and unheard, all of it was pushed out by a nameless, slippery panic. Hot and ungovernable, it rose inside her.

He was leaving.

'No.' Her hand closed around his wrist and he stopped. Everything stopped. Time stilled and they stood frozen, each absorbed in the other, rapt, transfixed, spellbound.

'No?' His voice was hoarse. He sounded dazed, disorientated.

'Don't go.'

He didn't kiss her. Instead, he kept staring at her, his stare and that shimmering thread of heat and possibility and punch-in-the-gut hunger pulsing through the silence, and then he reached out and wrapped his hand around her waist, pulling her closer.

And now he kissed her, and she tasted his need and frustration and something that might have been relief.

His fingers were moving now, pulling at her arms, unpeeling the sleeves from her body, and she felt the dress start to slip over her breasts.

The bodice had a built-in bra, and she shuddered as it grazed her nipples and suddenly she was bare from the waist up. She felt his breath hitch against her mouth and then his hands were cupping her breasts and she moaned softly as the tips hardened and she started to shake inside.

'I want you.'

It felt good to tell the truth, finally. To say what she wanted. What she needed. To be herself and not be ashamed.

'And I want you.' Her skin tightened, and every muscle in her body tensed as he leaned in and kissed her again, his hand pushing at the mass of fabric around her waist until it spilled onto the floor around her feet.

He stumbled back, his pupils flaring, and then he swore loudly.

She was naked now except for a tiny pair of panties, some stockings and her beautiful satin shoes.

His eyes were sharp with a hunger that left her in no doubt that he liked what he saw. She made as if to slip off one of her shoes but his hand caught her wrist.

'No...' He breathed out shakily. 'Keep them on. And the stockings.'

Her body twitched with need as he stared down at her and kept staring and staring and then he started to kiss her, hard, open-mouthed kisses that made heat blister up inside her pelvis. She moaned against his mouth, and he sat down on the stool and lifted her onto his lap, his hands sliding up to cup her breasts.

She shuddered against him, her nipples hardening beneath his thumbs, and then she reached for the zip of his trousers, and he groaned, his breath hot against her cheek as she freed him, her fingers moving over the smooth, swollen head of his erection, and now their breath hitched at the same time and then he was grabbing her hand and pressing down on himself as if he was trying to restrain himself.

But she didn't want him restrained.

She wanted him out of control. Ungoverned. Undone.

'Touch me,' she said hoarsely.

He grunted as she took his hand and pressed it against the damp silk between her thighs, shivering with need as he pushed the fabric to one side and slid first one then two fingers into her slick heat.

Now his eyes changed as she knew they would and he tugged her panties away from her body and lifted her up, and she reached down to guide him in.

He breathed in sharply, she did too, as he pushed in a couple of inches. Because she had forgotten what he felt like. The breadth of him and how hard and solid he was. Her hands gripped his shoulders and then she pushed herself down onto the length of him and his face stiffened and she moved against him, arching her back to offer her breasts.

She jerked forward as he sucked first one, then the other nipple into his mouth and she was grinding against him, her muscles tightening inside, trembling with impatience as she rubbed herself against his flexing body, chasing the heat and the friction. Her legs began to shake and then everything broke apart and she cried out as he drove upwards, thrusting inside her again and again and again as they both found their pleasure.

After, they sat panting, his body hot against hers and slick with sweat. Her body felt loose and tight all at once and it all felt so familiar and right.

She blinked, her eyes fixed on where the wedding dress lay on the carpet. It looked like a rose that had been knocked off mid-bloom by a summer storm or a chrysalis shed by a caterpillar as it became a butterfly. But she wasn't a rose or a butterfly in this man's eyes. She never had been.

To him, she was a means to an end.

And she had just had sex with him. Sweaty, urgent, breathless sex. And she had done it voluntarily, eagerly, as if she didn't know who he was or what he had done.

She stared at his chest, the line of his stomach, the iliac crests, the six-pack—or was it an eight-pack? Either way, he had a beautiful body. And just looking at him made her want to start touching him again, to curve her hand around the still hard length of him. To lose herself in the grip of his hands on her body and the weight of his body on hers and hurtle into that shuddering, unbound pleasure again and again and again.

Her chest heaved, and she sat up.

'What is it?' He shifted back, his eyes tracking down over the curve of her bottom as she got to her feet. 'What are you doing?'

He watched as she plucked a couple of tissues from a box on top of the dressing table and began wiping her thighs and then she walked swiftly to the dressing room and took one of the robes hanging on the rail.

'It's time to go,' she said as she came back into the room.

'Go,' he repeated softly. His eyes narrowed. 'We're not leaving until tomorrow.'

'For the honeymoon, yes,' she agreed. 'But I'm not talking about that. I'm talking about you needing to go to your room.'

'But I don't need to.'

'It's not about what you need. It's about what I want,' she said, using a tone that could have come straight out of her mother's mouth.

He scanned her face slowly. 'Wasn't that what just happened?' His green eyes felt like searchlights.

'Yes. Obviously, I wanted that, and now I would like you to leave.'

'This isn't some one-night stand. We're married.'

'I don't need reminding of that,' she snapped.

'You think? Maybe I'm wrong—unlike you, I've not been married before—but I was given to believe that married couples don't do the walk of shame after they have sex, even if it is only a few steps into the next room. And in case you've forgotten, this is our wedding night.'

She took a deep breath and took a step back.

'Why are you making this into such a big deal? We had sex. I'm sorry if you were expecting more but that's not going to happen. And nor are we spending the night together, so you need to leave.'

His eyes were dark and glossy like a jungle cat's and his muscles were bunching at his shoulders. 'You're unbelievable.' He gave a short, humourless bark of a laugh. 'You think I came back for this. For you. I didn't. But I'll take what just happened if it's on offer.'

She stared at him, mute with a shock that she knew was showing on her face, the hurt too.

'Get out,' she said finally.

'Why? You going to throw something else at me?'

He held her gaze, his face still as the air in the room quivered like lava. And it felt as if she were playing not with fire but an active volcano. Not that Vero would ever harm her physically. But there were other ways to cause pain.

'Fine, if you won't leave, then I will.'

His eyes narrowed and he made a grab for her as she turned away in one smooth movement. But his limbs were still loose and languid with

post-coital endorphins, and she reached the door
and slammed it, turning the key in the lock.

'Betty—' He swore loudly and the door trem-
bled as he slammed his hand against it. Then
again and again.

But it would hold. The doors were not just fire
resistant, they were bulletproof, and the locks
had a break time of three hours. Walking swiftly
across the room, she locked the door out into the
corridor. That too would hold.

Unlike her willpower apparently.

As Vero kept shouting her name, she curled
up on the sofa, shaking slightly. She had made
a mistake. A big one. But unlike tonight, there
was no handy connecting door that she could
bolt through to escape what she'd done. She was
married.

And the scandal of divorce meant that couldn't
change. But right now, she couldn't do this.
Couldn't pretend and lie. She needed space. She
needed somewhere to get her thoughts straight
otherwise she was not going to survive this marriage.

She needed somewhere safe to hide. Somewhere Vero wouldn't look.

And she knew just the place.

Getting to her feet, she opened the wardrobe.
Bella used this room so there were clothes neatly
folded on the shelves and she put on a pair of

jeans and a T-shirt, snatched up a baseball cap that her sister had brought back from their last trip to New York and then she sat down and waited.

Vero had stopped calling her name, but she waited another hour before she approached the door into the hallway. Her heart was pounding in her throat. She had no idea what she would do if he was waiting for her outside the room. But there was no one there and, clutching some of Bella's trainers, she ran lightly down the stairs.

There was a thin line of light along the horizon as she slipped into the garage and let herself into one of the cars. The key was on the charging tray and she started the engine, grateful that it was an electric vehicle.

Her heart thudded erratically as she waited for the security gates to lift, her gaze darting back to the door, expecting Vero's furious form to fly through it any moment. But then the gates were open and she accelerated up the ramp and out through the main gates onto the street, and freedom.

CHAPTER SIX

THE MORNING SUNLIGHT didn't so much wake Vero as nudge him out of a stupor. Reaching for his watch, he glanced at the face as he slid it onto his wrist. It was early: five-thirty. It felt earlier. Felt as if he hadn't slept at all, but he had. He knew that because he kept jerking awake from dreams where he was reaching out to grab Betty's arm only for her to slip through his fingers.

He sat up, his gaze pulling instantly to the connecting door between the two rooms as he remembered how he had hammered on it in the early hours of the morning shouting like a man possessed.

It had been a short-lived and unsuccessful siege—

The doors were security doors. He would need a battering ram to break through them and it was humiliating enough having to carry the memory of pleading with his new wife to open the door to him on his wedding night. He didn't need it to be accompanied by a soundtrack of police sirens.

It was definitely not his finest hour.

But then he'd still been coming down from his orgasm, and hers.

He felt his pulse twitch, picturing Betty's face, hearing that choking gasp she'd made as she'd contracted around him, and his own pleasure spiking and spilling out of him as they had shuddered against one another.

His fingers bit into the mattress.

He would be lying if he said that he hadn't wanted it to happen. Betty was his ex and there couldn't be many men who hadn't thought about sex with an ex. Only she wasn't his ex any more. She was his wife and truthfully, since that kiss at the palace, taking her mouth again, taking her, had been playing on repeat inside his head. Several times a day some version of that kiss and a myriad X-rated what-happened-nexts would pop into his head, usually at some completely inappropriate moment like during a meeting with his shareholders or when he was on a factory tour.

So yes, he had thought about it. But since the press conference to announce their engagement, they had only met once in the cathedral for the dress rehearsal, and she had been cool and composed.

And that hadn't changed at the ceremony or at

the wedding breakfast afterwards or even when they'd arrived here, and they had finally been alone. If anything, she'd felt even more out of reach. Despite the fact that she was wearing his ring.

He had wanted to punish her for that. To get under her skin in the same way that she managed so effortlessly to get under his.

And it had worked. They had argued and he'd had the satisfaction of watching her hurl priceless porcelain across the room.

Only then she had got stuck in her dress, and he should have left her to it. After all, it was her own fault. She had dismissed Elena and the rest of the household staff. She had dismissed him.

But then he had caught a glimpse of her face, and the panicky fumbling of her fingers, and he hadn't been able to leave.

And then everything had happened so fast. One minute he was unbuttoning her and trying not to let his gaze wander to the cut-out panel on the back of her dress and that tantalising glimpse of skin, and then it was done, and he was stepping backwards.

Which was when she'd reached out and touched his arm.

Because it was still there. That need. That blistering hunger that he'd never felt for any woman before or since. And there had been many 'befores' and 'sinces'. But Betty was different. Unique. Compelling.

Irresistible.

He breathed out unsteadily. Should he have stopped it? Probably. But he hadn't wanted to. He hadn't been able to tear his eyes from hers, much less wrest his hand from her body. He had been spellbound, dazed and light-headed, drowning in heat and hunger, and her.

And hell, they were on their honeymoon.

Picturing Betty's face when she'd gripped his wrist, he felt his body harden, his erection pressing painfully against the zip of his trousers. She had looked fierce, almost as if he was something essential to her, like water or oxygen.

The sex had felt like that too. Urgent. Necessary. Imperative, and it was fast. A dam breaking. And then it was over. Only he could remember thinking that couldn't be it. That things had only just got started. That it was simply a pause, a moment of reprieve to catch their breath before he got to do all the things he wanted to do to her.

His skin had still been twitching with pleasure, one hand curved around her waist, the other moving over her, dipping to where they were still joined. And then she had batted his fingers away and was pulling back, walking away to the dressing room.

Because she was done.

He gritted his teeth. *Done.*

His eyes snagged, magpie-like, on the glittering diamond necklace that she'd left behind, discarded casually as only a princess with a vault of jewels could do. Really, he shouldn't have been shocked by the ease with which she could walk away.

But it had been like a punch to the head. Actually, it had felt as if she were swarming him against the ropes, punching over and over.

And after complaining that it was hard to lie to the world, she had lied to his face. Telling him it had meant nothing to her. That if he'd come back for sex, then he'd made a huge mistake.

So yeah, it had stung. Knowing that, knowing she had just used him for sex.

Used him for sex? He swore. Yeah, because he hadn't wanted sex, wanted her?

The only possible answer to that question made his body tense so painfully that he jerked forward and rolled out of bed in one swift movement. He had been too furious and thwarted last night to get undressed but now, gazing down at his crumpled suit trousers and creased shirt, he felt a different frustration, the kind that had nothing to do with sex.

Because he shouldn't have said what he had.

'You think I came back for this. For you. I

didn't. But I'll take what just happened if it's on offer.'

The words reverberated inside his head, growing louder and uglier with every repetition.

He'd picked a fight with Betty because the Duke had snubbed him.

The tightness in his chest seemed to be spreading through his limbs.

He'd known the Duke would be there. Had specifically requested a large-scale wedding in order to guarantee his biological father's presence. And yet bumping into him on the dance floor like that had knocked him off balance not just literally but metaphorically. Probably because he was already on edge after watching Betty being spun round by her father and all the memories that had provoked—

So many lies in one room.

Too many.

And they were, all of them, still lying now. He thought back to the moment when his father's eyes had met his. The Duke had bowed to Betty but when he'd greeted Vero, the slight tilt of his head could have been directed at one of the standing candelabras.

And he'd hated how that made him feel. Hated that it even had the power to make him feel anything. It was humiliating. He felt humiliated and diminished, and also guilty that Tommasino wasn't there, and it had been easy to blame Betty and the pragmatic, focused way she had been trying to clean herself with tissues.

As if he were something to be wiped away.

It was all such a mess, and someone needed to sort it. He needed to sort it. Not with an apology, never that. More a reset.

This marriage might be fake but there was no point in pretending that the history between them hadn't happened. But he was prepared to put it behind him and if he could do that then she could too, and then she could stop fighting what she so obviously wanted. What they both wanted.

He tucked his shirt into his trousers. His feet were bare, and he needed a shave but that could wait. First, he would talk to Betty, make it clear how this was going to work from now on. He spotted the necklace, and picked it up. It would serve as a peace offering.

He tapped on the interconnecting door. There was no response and when he tried the handle it was still locked so he made his way to the other door...

It was ajar.

He pushed it open. The room was empty.

His heart beat irregularly against his ribs as he checked the bathroom but that too was empty. He glanced back at the bed, his breath congealing in his throat. The bed didn't even look as if it had been slept in.

The walls shuddered in and out of focus as he stared around the silent room and then he turned and walked swiftly back through the door and towards the stairs. The villa was silent and there was no evidence of any staff on site although he could see the uniformed security guards standing stiffly at their posts. Shoving the necklace into his pocket, he strode from room to room, moving quietly but with purpose, but there was no sign of Betty.

Finally, he found himself in the underground garage. His eyes moved over the three bays. There were cars parked in two of them.

He felt his stomach lurch in his throat as he gazed at the third bay. It was empty, and he knew why.

Betty had taken the car. And he'd lay odds that she wasn't coming back.

'Excuse me, Your Highness.'

Betty glanced up as one of the maids darted forward to clear away her plate and then she smiled. It was her first real smile in weeks. Leaning back, she gazed up at the silvery foliage and breathed in deeply. And it was all thanks to Ponza.

She was having a late breakfast-cum-lunch out

on the terrace behind the Villa Giglio. She had arrived in the early hours of the morning and, stepping off the speedboat, she had felt relief and gratitude. Here she was not at risk of making a fool of herself.

It might only be for a couple of days—she would have to join Vero in the Caribbean eventually—but in the meantime, she could get her head straight, formulate some ground rules for how their marriage would work.

It was what she should have done the moment she'd agreed to marry him, but she had been sleepwalking towards the wedding. Going through the motions. Thinking was beyond her.

But she could think here.

Situated roughly midway between Naples and Rome, Ponza was little more than a dot in the Tyrrhenian Sea, small enough that if you were looking at a map you might think it a stray spot of ink.

It was the largest of the Pontine islands, an archipelago that made her think of the breadcrumbs dropped by Hansel and Gretel to find their way back home. Which was ironic because when Odysseus stopped on Ponza on his way back from Troy he ended up staying a year, seduced by the sorceress Circe and her magical potions.

But for her Ponza was more than just a stopping place. The Prince's Palace might be her official home but the Villa Giglio on the island of Ponza was where she had always felt at home. Home was where the heart was and for all his faults her grandfather had the biggest heart of anyone she knew.

Tilting her head back, she gazed up at the olive tree, watching the branches move in the sea breeze. Here, she and Bella had been free to play like normal children. They had not been on display. Not been critiqued and judged and, in her case, found wanting. They had climbed trees and swum in the sea and played hide and seek in the orchards.

And now it was hers. Bella had been given the apartment in Paris, but the Villa Giglio belonged to Betty. It was the perfect bolt-hole. Situated at the southern tip of the island, it had a jetty and a private beach, which was so surrounded by rocks that it was practically a lagoon. And because her grandfather had charmed the island's residents, they were sympathetic to Betty's need for privacy and so she was never bothered in the street. Not that she went out much.

The joy of Villa Giglio was that it was truly the only place in the world where she got to be herself. Not a princess. Not the heir to the throne. Not the wife of a man who didn't like her, much less love her.

Just Betty.

Here, the sun was always shining, the sky was blue, and she could breathe. It was addictive and intoxicating.

'Excuse me, Your Highness.' This time it was the housekeeper, Mariangela. 'I wondered if you might prefer to have a later lunch today?'

Mariangela hadn't so much as blinked when Betty had arrived on her own at a quarter past one in the morning and this was, she knew, the closest the housekeeper would get to referring to the matter. Mariangela had worked for her grandfather and embodied discretion and old-school loyalty.

'You know, I might skip lunch. I'll dine earlier this evening. Have there been any messages for me, Mariangela?' she added after a moment, casually as if the thought had just occurred to her. Or that was what she was aiming for, but she could feel the heat rising up over her face just as if she were sitting in direct sunlight rather than beneath the canopy of leaves.

'No, Your Highness.'

Which meant that her father didn't know what had happened.

But Vero did. He must do by now.

Her stomach somersaulted. Stupid, she told herself. Because Vero couldn't have made it any clearer last night that she meant nothing to him.

Although he was happy to have sex if it was on offer.

On offer.

Now her cheeks felt as though they were on fire.

She remembered the shiver that had zigzagged through her body as Vero had gripped her waist and kissed her. It had been a rough kiss, a kiss of hunger and release.

No words had been spoken. But none had been needed.

He knew what she wanted. Knew her body as a migrating bird knew the ley lines of the earth. He had mapped every inch of her skin with his fingers and tongue. And she had done the same with him.

It had felt like coming home, and danger all at once.

Her eyes tracked upwards, following a sweep of cirrocumulus clouds in the otherwise empty blue sky.

Except there was nothing homely about Vero. He might look every inch the urbane business titan, but he was dangerous.

Not violent or abusive. Never that.

But he made her reckless. Made her forget that her judgement was flawed. But that was the trouble with sex. When it felt right, as it did with Vero, it did something to your brain. Took the brakes off. And when that happened there was collateral damage.

Which was why she was here, in Ponza, not halfway across the Atlantic Ocean in Vero's private jet en route to her honeymoon at his villa on Turks and Caicos.

She wondered what he was telling people.

But that was a Vero problem.

This whole wedding had been cooked up between him and her father. If at any point either one of them had asked for her opinion she would have told them that she didn't want time alone on an island with the man who had broken her heart and who was currently in the process of pressing on the imperfectly repaired cracks.

But nobody had asked her opinion or required any input on her part. So, Vero could deal with any fallout, and she was going to spend a couple of days here doing absolutely nothing for anyone but herself.

She spent the rest of the morning doing precisely that, starting off in a hammock strung between two olive trees and then wandering through the orchard down to where the estate jutted out into the Tyrrhenian, letting her gaze drift out across the shimmering aquamarine water to where it became a thin dark line at the sky's edge. There was so much blue. It was like drowning but without the struggle. Right now, that seemed like a win.

But it was time to get back. She walked slowly through the orchard, stopping here and there to test the ripeness of the fruit. Every step was done at her pace. She was pleasing herself and it felt wonderful.

Her body stiffened reflexively, and she squinted through her sunglasses. Someone was walking towards her. No doubt it was one of the staff. She raised her hand and waved as the dark, indistinct shape grew sharper. And then her hand froze in mid-air and the tenacious, exuberant beauty of the day collided with reality and shock washed through her in waves.

No.

Not him. It couldn't be him. Not here. She couldn't take it in, couldn't understand how he could be here in Ponza. Slowly she slid off her glasses, half hoping that they were distorting her vision in some way.

They weren't.

And even though she didn't want to, she found herself marvelling at the way he moved. There was both an elegance and a fluidity to it, like a dancer. Only there was also a sense of purpose in the rippling muscle and, even from a distance, she could feel the incredible focus of his green-eyed gaze.

Less dancer, she thought, her pulse skittering forward like a startled rabbit. More panther.

Was this how Circe had felt seeing Odysseus approach?

Vero stopped in front of her.

The sun was on her face so it was hard to see his expression but then he shifted to block out the light and her heart beat out a drum roll of panic and irritation, and something she didn't want to acknowledge, much less feel. Because he looked good.

Her breath snatched and she felt the leaves blur around her into a mass of swirling silver that matched the fog in her brain.

By good she meant every kind of right.

There was no mirror to hand, but she knew that her face was probably flushed and possibly sweaty from the heat of the sun and she could feel a slight stickiness around her mouth from where she had been eating figs straight from the tree.

But aside from a graze of dark stubble, Vero looked exactly as he had in the cathedral although his clothes, as befitted a man on his honeymoon, were less formal. Gone was the dark, tailored suit and made-to-measure shirt. Instead, he was wearing cream chinos and a green polo that was a shade darker than his irises and clung to his body as if he'd been shrink-wrapped.

Her eyes slid over him jerkily, snagging on the stripe of muscles bisecting his torso.

She felt it beat through her blood then. Anger. Hot and furious because what gave him the right to do this? To turn up looking so distractingly enticing. To turn up at all.

This was *her* home. She had the deeds. She paid the household bills out of her pocket. But it was more than just a home. It was her sanctuary.

A safe space where she could be herself or at least try and find out who that was after so long just simply being what was required of her. And this marriage had made her feel even less solid and sure of herself.

All she had wanted was time alone. Time to regroup, to bolster herself against this life she hadn't chosen. He couldn't even give her that, she thought, resentment twisting her stomach.

But she was ready for him.

'How did you find me?'

'Your father.' His eyes rested on her face. He sounded calm, but his eyes told a different story. 'Not intentionally. He doesn't know you're here. He let slip something at the wedding. It was lucky I remembered. Your staff were not helpful at all.'

'It's called loyalty, Vero. It's not a concept you understand.'

He stared at her in silence, regrouping maybe

or more likely just making her wait for his reply. Tilting up her chin, she glared at him.

'What are you doing here?'

'I think that's my line, Your Highness?' he said softly, but the smile that accompanied his words was hard and dangerous.

He stared at her in silence for a long, level moment as if he was considering his response.

'You left something at the house,' he said finally. Her muscles tensed as he reached into his pocket and as he pulled out his hand, she saw a flash of diamonds.

She lifted a hand to her throat. 'My necklace.'

'That too.' He held her gaze. 'But I was actually talking about me. You do realise we are supposed to be on our way to Turks and Caicos?'

She tilted back her head. 'I do.'

'I do?' Pausing, his smile hardened into a frown. 'I do. That sounds familiar?' He shook his head now, doing mock confusion. 'Oh, yeah, I remember. I said it yesterday in the cathedral when we got married. You said it too.' His smile vanished and she saw the anger in his eyes flare and, beneath it, the smouldering, wounded male pride.

'Although that appears to have slipped your mind, unless you have some other, compelling reason for leaving me to go on our honeymoon alone?'

'Let me see.' Now it was her turn to feign confusion. 'How about not wanting to spend any more time alone with you than I have to? Does that count?'

His eyes narrowed. 'Don't play games with me, Betty.'

'You think this is a game?' She held his gaze. 'Games are for pleasure. I'm just doing my duty.'

'Is that what you think you're doing here?' She felt a jolt of heat as he took a step towards her. 'And what about your father? Do you think he'd agree with your interpretation? Perhaps we should surprise him? Give him a call, find out?'

There was no need, she thought, trying not to picture her father's cool, disdainful expression. He wouldn't be surprised. Whatever she did, his response was always the same. The only variable was the extent of his disappointment and how long it lasted.

What was a surprise was the sharp, tangible pain she felt knowing Vero would betray her to her father.

'Be my guest.' She took a step backwards, turning on her heel. 'You can have a nice little chat with him because right now I'm not ready to talk with you, which is—'

What happened next was such a shock that by the time she had processed it Vero had caught her arm, stopping her mid-flight, the impetus spinning her round, and was already scooping her into his arms.

She fought his grip, pitting her strength against his until they reached the villa and then she stilled, seething with fury as he strode through the house, past Mariangela and one of the open-mouthed maids, and up the stairs to her room.

He dumped her on the bed without ceremony and she flew to her feet, her hands curling into fists. It was a long way from being the perfect princess, but she didn't care.

'How dare you?'

They were inches apart, their breath staccato, and his eyes were the darkest they had ever been, and she could feel them pulling her under, feel herself flowing towards him—

She slammed her hands against his chest.

'How dare you humiliate me like that?'

'Oh, I dare, Princess.' He caught her wrists, holding her at arm's length, his grip tight enough that she couldn't break free. 'I'm not some footman you can ignore. I'm your husband. And frankly you don't get to talk about humiliation, not after that stunt you pulled.'

'You got off lightly.' She sounded breathless now, as if she were running, not fighting, and for a moment she wished she were.

The tendons in his hands were taut with the

effort of holding her still. Or holding himself
back. 'You walked out on me. On our wedding
night. Just skipped off into the sunset alone,
without so much as a word—'

She stared at him, stung and stunned not just
by his words but by his evident belief that they
were justified.

'And you plotted this whole marriage behind
my back,' she said after a moment.

He ignored her. 'You left me to come up with
some explanation for why my wife had vanished
into thin air.'

Her arms were tiring now and she let them go
limp, and after a breath he let go of her.

'I'm sure you thought of something. Telling
bare-faced lies is your forte.'

His irises blazed, glittering like gemstones
against the black of his pupils, but she held her
ground. 'I don't see why you care. Our marriage
isn't real, ergo this honeymoon isn't real either.'
He hadn't even proposed, she realised, a lump
filling her throat. He had given her a ring but
had simply handed her the box and let her slide
it onto her finger.

For a moment neither of them spoke and she
knew that the silence filling the room must be
taut and uncomfortable, but her pulse was so
loud in her ears that she couldn't hear anything.
Breathing in, she stared past his shoulder at the

square of limpid blue sea through the window, trying to calm herself. If only she were Circe, she could give him a potion and he would be hers to command, and she could command him to leave.

Would she though? She hated that the question, the need to even ask it, made her heart beat in her throat.

'We have to have a honeymoon,' he said brusquely after a moment. 'Surely you can see that.'

'I do. I did. I just—'

All she had wanted was a couple of days to clear her head but why should she explain herself? Besides, any explanation would expose her to that glittering green gaze and reveal just how badly he had hurt her.

'Then you also know that it has to look real. Making that happen will be better for everyone.'

Her stomach knotted. Better for everyone was what people said when something went their way. But nothing could ever be better for everyone.

'Better for you, you mean,' she said bitterly. And for her father too. But it was bad enough that Vero didn't care about her feelings. He didn't need to know that Prince Vittorio had no qualms about sacrificing his daughter to a man he had previously despised.

Vero shrugged. 'Better for Malaspina too. And the House of Marchetta. Which is why you're marrying me, isn't it?'

She could feel Vero's gaze on her face, cool and intent as though, if he stared hard enough, he could see her thoughts passing through her head. She forced her eyes up to meet his.

'Why else would I ever marry a man like you?'

'Why indeed?' There was no emotion in his voice. 'Perhaps if you're struggling it might help to focus on your responsibilities,' he said then. 'You need heirs.'

It didn't help to be reminded. What was more, she didn't need to be reminded. Her responsibilities were with her constantly. And theoretically she understood, had always understood, that she had to sacrifice her wishes and the paths she wanted to follow, to deny what she needed, in order to ensure the security of her family and the prosperity of her country and its people.

But increasingly it had felt like a crushing weight smothering her.

The only times she felt free and able to breathe were here on Ponza, only now Vero had taken that from her too.

'I don't need you to give me advice, particularly not when it comes to my responsibilities,' she snapped.

'So, what do you need?' His gaze was suddenly intent so that the air between them seemed to soften treacherously, and she bit the inside of her mouth hard enough that it hurt, hurt enough to make her snap straight into a forward-weighted stance like a boxer squaring up her opponent.

Because whatever her body might be telling her, that was what he was.

'For you to leave.'

'You know that's not going to happen. I'm not going anywhere, and if you try to run away again, I'll let the press know that we're here, and then your little bolt-hole will be crawling with paparazzi.'

She flinched. 'You wouldn't do that.' Unlike its more cosmopolitan, better-known neighbour Capri, Ponza remained happily under the radar.

He looked at her for one long, excruciating moment. 'Try me,' he said coolly and the calmness in his voice knocked the breath from her chest.

When her father had threatened to marry Bella to the Duke, she had told herself that marriage to Vero was worth it to save her sister from the fate she had suffered at the same age. It had felt like the right sacrifice.

But now...

'You're a monster.'

His unyielding mouth was a hard line, his expression flat and unforgiving. 'You didn't think that last night.'

Heat burned in her cheeks and she turned her head. She didn't want to look at him. Didn't want to have anything to do with him.

'I wasn't thinking last night, I was—'

Wanting. Needing. Craving.

His gaze sharpened into a point of such intensity that it seemed to puncture her skin and leave her open and exposed. Why else would it feel as if he could read her mind?

She cleared her throat. 'It was a lot—the day, all the people, the expectations. I was tense and—'

Her heart hammered against her ribs as his pupils fattened. 'Yeah, sex is good for that,' he said slowly. 'Our sex anyway.' He seemed taken aback by that admission, or maybe by the fact that he had made it unprompted.

Our sex. *Our. Sex.*

She stared at him sideswiped, unhinged, feeling his words fizz against her skin like pulses of electricity, and she hated her brain for not policing her synapses better. Hated her body for being so susceptible to the idea of 'our' and 'sex' when it came to Vero, and she knew that she couldn't survive this marriage, couldn't survive him unless she drew a line, here, now.

Lifting her chin, she shook her head. 'Having sex like we did last night is a complication we don't need.'

Her heart beat erratically as his eyes found hers. 'On the contrary. I would say it's non-negotiable. How else are you planning on producing an heir?'

'You're not listening to me,' she said as evenly as she could. 'I didn't say we wouldn't have sex. We just won't have it randomly—'

He frowned. 'Randomly?'

The tension in his voice was suffusing the air so that it crackled against her skin. But this gravitational pull between them had to be managed. Once upon a time she might have dreamed of marriage freeing her from her suffocating life at the palace, but this marriage to Vero made her feel breathless all the time.

Her throat worked around her breath now as she pictured him, his hand tightening in her hair as he was overwhelmed by his shuddering orgasm.

She needed to break this spell. What she needed was a protocol, a ruling that would permit no exceptions. That was how she'd been raised. It was what she knew.

It was not lost on her, the irony of her wanting what she had chafed against for so long, but she needed to do something to expel Vero from her head.

'You know, spontaneously. For pleasure.' She was speaking quickly now, wanting to get the words out. 'I've downloaded an app so I can work out when I'm ovulating and maximise the chances of getting pregnant, and that's when we'll have sex. Then, and only then.'

CHAPTER SEVEN

VERO DIDN'T REPLY, didn't so much as blink, but abruptly the temperature in the room plummeted as if their argument had triggered a hyper-localised disaster-movie-style flash-freeze.

'Let me get this right. You downloaded an app so you can work out when you're ovulating and that's when we'll have sex. Just then, and only then,' he repeated, tilting his head back as if he was considering her words.

'Yeah, that's not going to happen.' His voice was quiet and unwavering but there was a hoarseness to it that made her take a steadying breath.

'It is exactly what's going to happen,' she said, trying her hardest to ignore the panic fluttering against her ribs. 'Surely you weren't expecting us to be lovers.'

His gaze snapped to her face and she felt it like a flame licking her skin. As if he were actually touching her. His open mouth hot against her throat. His hand tightening against her waist as she came apart uncontrollably around him…

'You're my wife, so weirdly I was expecting a conversation, not some royal decree that I present myself in your bedroom when summoned, solely for the purpose of breeding.'

'Funny, I never had you down for being melodramatic.'

'And I never had you down for being delusional.'

She had been delusional once. Nine years ago, when Vero had returned after a three-month internship in America, and the green-eyed boy she knew had disappeared. In his place was a man who made the air shimmer brighter than the sun.

He was dazzling, and like a moth she had allowed herself to be fascinated by the light. She had let him get close. Let herself believe that he had seen the woman beneath the crown and liked her, loved her.

Stupid, she thought. Deluded.

But not any more. It was humiliating to admit it, but this was something she couldn't lie about, at least not to herself, and the truth was that she was vulnerable where Vero was concerned. Too susceptible to that catch-and-trap green gaze of his. Just signing off on a sexual relationship with him without adding in some checks and measures would be an act of self-harm comparable to voluntarily wading through lava.

But she needed heirs, which was why there had to be rules.

'Hard to be delusional over something so transparently transactional. Which is what this marriage is. There's a trade-off. You get your title.' She couldn't keep the bitterness out of her voice, but she forced herself to keep speaking. 'I get an heir. So, we need to have sex. Only I would rather that there be less of it, and that it serves a specific function.'

'Can you hear the words coming out of your mouth?' He stared at her incredulously. 'Have you forgotten what happened last night in Milan?'

She tried to swallow but couldn't. Of course she hadn't forgotten. Every feverish kiss, the feel of his hand between her thighs, his other hand tightening in her hair, it was all there inside her head, pressing forward. And she was like the little Dutch boy with her finger in the dam wall, trying to hold it all back.

But what if by holding back she was making things worse? Vero was like a virus in her blood. Perhaps what she needed was to sweat him out. For a moment she imagined how it would feel to give in to her need for him. Imagined the varied and many acts it would take to work him out of her system and the serenity that would follow.

What if? What if?

The question echoed inside her head, and she felt a stab of irritation at her indecisiveness. But then her judgement had been proven to be flawed before and with such appalling consequences.

'What happened in Milan is exactly why there needs to be rules—'

'And you expect me to believe that's what you want?'

'It is what I want,' she said quickly, but then she shivered and his mouth, that indecently seductive mouth of his, curled into a shape that was part sneer, part snarl.

'Hasn't there been enough lies?' His voice vibrated with a complex dissonance of the raw and the restrained. 'Can't you just be honest about wanting this?'

Honest? She wanted to scream. Throw more things at his beautiful face. Instead, she said crisply, 'Thanks to you I can't be honest about anything. You breed lies and now you've turned my life into one too.'

'Then we're even.'

Her stomach lurched and she opened her mouth to protest but he was already speaking.

'You might be able to fool everyone else with

that butter-wouldn't-melt-in-your-mouth smile, but I know you, Betty, and you've wanted me ever since I walked back into your father's palace. You wanted me at the airfield and on the steps of the cathedral and you want me now—'

Her heart was racing, and she felt a shiver rake through her almost as if his hands were moving over her body and she were rushing towards that splintering rush of pleasure.

It would be so easy to surrender...

She shrugged. 'I know this must be hard for you, Vero, but sometimes in life, we have to make compromises.'

If he recognised his words, he gave no sign.

'I'm not agreeing to this.' His voice was cool and measured again but his eyes were a dark, glittering green like the lightning that accompanied the ash clouds above a volcanic eruption.

Tough, she thought, her own eyes narrowing in on his beautiful, symmetrical face. The resolve she'd felt earlier, the need to make a stand, hardened inside her like quenched steel because it wasn't a coincidence that she had swapped living with one single-minded, ruthless man who wanted things entirely his way, for life with another. The only difference was that this was married life.

But this wasn't simply about her father or Vero. It was about her, and she was done with being the perfect princess. Done with letting men jerk her strings to make her dance until her body ached and her feet were blistered and all the while smiling through the pain. Done with being weak.

'You mean like I didn't agree to this marriage. Yet here we are, married.'

His jaw twitched. 'Except, you did agree, Princess Bettina.'

Yes, she had agreed because the alternative was to sacrifice her baby sister to a loveless marriage of convenience and the stifling, early widowhood that would inevitably follow. 'I was given no choice,' she said tightly.

No choice.

Vero almost laughed. What did Betty know about having no choice?

She had never been evicted from her home or sacked from her job and been powerless to do anything about it. She didn't understand how it felt to offer love and be rejected, be deemed unworthy, because she was a princess who was loved unconditionally by thousands of her subjects. She didn't know what it felt like to have been written out of one's own history, excised from a bloodline, spurned and scorned from birth.

From before birth, he thought, his breath suddenly jagged edged. It still stung just as it had all those years ago, not just discovering that his whole life was a lie but the efforts his biological father had made to distance himself from his bastard child. And was still making.

Remembering how the Duke's eyes had shuttered on the dance floor, he felt so angry that when he spoke he made no effort to soften his tone.

'Do you know how unbelievably spoiled you sound?'

Her eyes jerked to his face, the pupils widening just as if he'd slapped her, but he didn't care. 'Choice is a luxury. It's earned, not inherited. But what do you know about earning anything? Never mind a silver spoon, your entire life was gilt-wrapped and handed to you at birth. Nothing has ever been out of reach. People go out of their way to try and make you happy. And they worship you. Do you know how rare that is? How fortunate you are?'

Taking her lack of response for assent, he continued.

'Then what exactly have you done with all those opportunities and all that favour and adoration, Princess Bettina?'

There was a short, ugly silence.

Betty was staring at him, only she didn't look like herself. That luminosity beneath her skin had vanished as if a candle had been snuffed out and seeing her like that blew out the flame of his anger.

She shook her head slowly. 'You know nothing about my life. You know nothing about me. And I know nothing about you. But I think that's probably for the best given that the more I get to know you, the less I like.'

He wanted to pull her close then and kiss her until she melted into him, and he could prove inarguably that he knew her better than she knew herself. But she looked so brittle he was scared that if he touched her, she might break into a thousand pieces.

Instead, he turned and walked back out of her room and through the house and out into the sunshine that seemed overtly, mockingly cheerful in comparison to the dull ache inside his chest.

The perfect dive was a blend of poise, power and precision. There was no time to blink or breathe as you plummeted into the water.

Stretching out his hand, Vero gazed down into the clear, rippling water. He'd dived off cliffs before but not with this level of emotion churning inside him. It was risky but right now he needed that rush of adrenaline to swamp his anger and frustration with Betty, and himself.

He was supposed to be pulling the strings but

instead he'd finally been shipwrecked after days on stormy seas.

Releasing the rock he was holding, he watched it fall, tracking its path, his brain filling with equations for velocity and distance as he watched its descent, calculating how long it would take to hit the surface and how long it would therefore take him.

Sometimes you had to let things go.

He bent his knees and pushed off, soaring forward, his arms up and over his head, his elbows pressed against his ears, thumbs locked together.

As he hit the water, his world went blue and then he pushed up towards the light, breaking the surface tension and breathing in sharply.

But Betty wasn't one of those things you let go.

He swam then, needed to swim to counteract the tension and the rush of adrenaline that thought produced, cutting through the waves, momentarily lulled by the freedom of movement and the easy rhythm of his body. Finally, he pulled himself onto the spray-soaked rock, smoothing his wet hair back against the contours of his skull.

His arm was bleeding. He must have scraped it on a rock. But the blood was nowhere near as shocking as that conversation with Betty in her bedroom. That had blown his mind.

Afterwards, maybe an hour later, they had eaten dinner together and by then her emotions had defused and she had recovered her poise. Which was a relief, at first. He hadn't liked seeing her so shaken and he'd felt uncomfortably out of his depth.

But it also needled him that she could contain her feelings like that. Conceal herself from him. And he kept remembering what she said about his not knowing her and he hated that, despite his having married her, she could still defy him, still stay out of reach and opaque.

That wasn't part of the plan.

Exiting the water, he pulled on a T-shirt and some flip-flops and made his way back up to the villa.

Then again, what worked on paper often stalled and stumbled when confronted by the limitations of reality. Over a decade working in the automotive industry had taught him that.

But his marriage to Betty had been deceptively simple to arrange.

There had been no real negotiations. Vittorio had not just offered him the title of duke; he had insisted on it. But then money was a great emollient, and the Prince needed money. Not that he'd shared that fact with Vero, but then Vero hadn't revealed that Frederico had already blabbed to him about the Marchetta finances, so they were equal.

His mouth twisted. Equal. It was all he'd ever wanted to be, and he'd got lost in the feeling and stupidly assumed that everything else, and by everything else he meant Betty, would fall into line.

That now seemed both ludicrous and naive.

His eyes moved over the terrace. The loungers were empty but there was an indent in one of the cushions and Betty's book lay open on it, its pages fluttering open in the breeze as if it had been discarded in a hurry.

Which no doubt it had the moment she heard him approaching.

He felt his jaw tighten. It was a game they were playing. A cross between catch me if you can and hide and seek and he was pretty sure her staff were in on it. He could see no other explanation for why his wife was always one step ahead of him. And why, when she finally emerged from the shadows, they were never alone.

It was driving him insane. All of it.

Not only had his father looked through him as if he were a servant, but his wife had also reduced his status to that of a stallion brought in to cover a mare and was currently avoiding his company so successfully that he was starting to wonder if she led a parallel life as an intelligence agent.

But he hadn't become the CEO of one of the biggest global automotive businesses on the planet by chance.

Nobody at the top had got there without stamping on a few fingers. It came with the territory. They knew right from wrong but engaged in immoral or sometimes illegal behaviour anyway. Sabotaging or intimidating their rivals, using their wealth and influence to get their own way.

But, as his mother used to say, *'Si prendono più mosche col miele che con l'aceto.'* Honey caught more flies than vinegar.

It was time to go back to the drawing board. He wasn't going to be kept standing at stud for weeks at a time until Betty decided it was time for him to service her. He wanted what they'd had nine years ago, what they'd had in Milan, and so, he was sure, did Betty. They just needed some time alone without a phalanx of her staff chaperoning her and then it would happen. He felt a surge of desire. She would reach for him, and he pictured her hand touching his face, his chest, his—

His eyes narrowed. Mariangela had appeared on the terrace.

Raising his hand in greeting, he strolled towards the housekeeper, a smile melting onto his face.

'*Ciao*, Mariangela—'

'Your Grace.' Smiling politely, she bobbed a curtsey.

'It's a beautiful day, isn't it?'

'We are blessed.' She nodded. 'Is there something I can help you with, Your Grace?'

To the right of the housekeeper, Vero could see the indent in the cushion and his body tensed, painfully.

He nodded. 'As a matter of fact, there is…'

Watching her staff clear the plates away from the table, Betty sat stiff-backed in her chair, her mind a whirlpool of confusion and resentment.

She had taken a stand, finally, and arguably too late because Vero was still her husband. But she had done it. She had pushed back against the juggernaut that was Vero Farnese and given him a taste of what it felt like to be powerless. And it felt good.

Less than she'd expected, but it was something to have wiped that complacent expression off Vero's handsome face.

Afterwards they'd dined together. A truly uncomfortable experience but she hadn't let on and, more importantly, she had made sure that they were never alone. Actually, that wasn't true. She hadn't said anything to Mariangela or any of the staff, but then she hadn't needed to. As her grandfather always used to say, what marked out a good housekeeper was that rare mix of intuition and anticipation of what was required.

Which was how she had managed to avoid being alone with Vero.

Until this evening. And she was still trying to work out what had changed, and how she had ended up eating a romantic supper out on the terrace with a pink and yellow ombre sunset as a backdrop.

Mariangela glided forward as the final piece of cutlery was whisked away. 'Would you like some coffee, Your—?'

She cut across the housekeeper's question. 'No, that won't—'

'Yes, please, Mariangela.' Vero spoke at the same time, leaning across the table to wrap his hand around Betty's. 'We'll take it in the lounge...unless, of course, you're ready to go up, *cara*?'

She gave him a glacial smile. 'Not at all. I feel wide awake, as it happens.'

'Perhaps we should skip the coffee, then,' he said, feigning concern.

'Aren't you sweet to worry about me?' She gave him a smile that didn't reach her eyes. 'But there's really no need. I don't get affected by caffeine.'

It was like a dance. Except that not only did

she have to follow her partner's lead, she was also having to redirect him and all without making it so that they ended up colliding with one another.

Her pulse twitched.

Dancing was hard enough but there were rules about where you could touch and the distance between you. Whereas a collision...

She wasn't talking about a physical collision, but her brain went there anyway, which was both predictable and proof that she was right to create a framework for their relationship, the sex part anyway. She needed distance from Vero. Not just the spatial kind but inside her head where the boundaries were less defined and he was always so close.

Too close. He needed to be contained.

Was that possible?

Her gaze moved briefly to his beautiful, sculpted face. He had been furious earlier but maybe now he'd had time to cool off, he could be reasonable.

Reasonable? Her heart, which had been beating steadily until then, began to race as she got to her feet.

Vero wasn't sure how she did it but Betty managed to extricate her hand from his, rise like Cleopatra from her palanquin and was following Mariangela back into the villa before he'd even got to his feet. Once again, he found himself having to chase after her.

And despite his irritation, he found himself admiring her poise. It came so naturally to her, but he had learned the hard way that emotions were better kept in check.

For a moment, he was back in his birth father's palatial villa watching a police officer cuff Tommasino, the wild, choking anger that had propelled him there swamped now by the slippery panic building in his chest. That day had taught him a lot about the world, and the man who had fathered him and the man who was his father in every way except genetically. But most of all it had taught him that emotions were dangerous and so he had learned how to manage them.

In a world where he was helpless and silenced, exercising a rigid control over his feelings was a power of sorts.

And that ability to stay focused, to not get distracted by his emotions or other people's, had been the best business lesson of all. That it overlapped into his private life had never been a problem.

Until now.

Vero's eyes moved to Betty's face. The mask was back in place. Only a slight smokiness to her eyes and that pulse beating somewhat erratically against the smooth skin of her throat suggested that she might be a fraction less composed than she appeared.

He watched, torn between irritation and amusement as she skirted past the sofas and armchairs to feign interest in the view of the sunset through the French doors. It was a beautiful view, he conceded, dropping down onto a pale green velvet-covered sofa.

But he had a better one. His eyes moved over her light curves and he felt his body respond with humbling predictability.

It was like being held hostage.

His one consolation was that she felt the same way. She had to feel the same way.

He pulled his gaze away from Betty's silhouette and stared around the room.

The Prince's Palace and the Marchetta residence in Milan were one of a kind. High-ceilinged, opulent, ostentatious, with their layers of gilt and marble and bronze, but the Villa Giglio had an entirely different vibe. Comfort was key. Furniture was fit for purpose and rather than being smothered in oversized portraits of illustrious ancestors, the cream-coloured walls were bare aside from a striking canvas of a woman.

'Who's the artist?'

Betty turned now as he'd hoped she would, her grey eyes tracking across the room to the painting. 'Marie Laurencin.'

'Interesting choice.' His eyes narrowed on the woman gazing back at him from the canvas. 'Yours?'

He watched her walk towards the painting and stop in front of it.

'My grandfather's originally, but I always loved it.'

Watching her talk, he realised that it was the first time she hadn't been on high alert since he'd walked into the sitting room at the Prince's Palace. And he found himself relaxing too and not just because he was able to watch that mouth of hers without needing a justification. That seriousness and her obvious sincerity mesmerised him now just as they had nine years ago.

Tricked him, he corrected himself, and the memory of his stupidity, then and now, made his own voice rough as he gestured to the painting. 'It suits the room.'

She turned back to face him, and he took the opportunity to let his gaze roam over her small, high breasts and the slight uptilt of her chin.

'I'm guessing it's not to your taste.' Her response was accompanied by one of those grey-eyed stares and a silence swelling with quivering bow-flexing tension.

Vero stared assessingly at the woman in the painting. Despite the pastel colour palette and demure clothing, there was something arresting about her eyes, something provocative. She might be presented as soft, submissive even, but beneath the composure there was fire.

Without warning, his brain switched focus from the painted woman with the taunting gaze to the real-life woman standing across the room and he found himself remembering Betty's fire, and the way she had melted into him, her mouth seeking his to kiss him hungrily with those bee-stung lips of hers…

For a few undulating moments he forgot how to speak. 'You guessed wrongly,' he said after a moment, getting to his feet and walking towards her. 'I like it a lot. There's something subversive there.'

'Yes, that's right.'

She glanced up at him sharply, her eyes widening with shock and recognition, and it was so intoxicating to be the focus of her attention in a good way that the world tilted momentarily on its axis.

'You have to lift the veil but it's there,' he said softly.

Her pupils flared and her lips did something complicated as if she was about to speak then forgot what she was going to say and his brain blanked as he felt her silence inside his bones, and, more critically, low in his groin.

'What happened to your arm?'

He glanced down. 'It's just a scratch. I was diving off the cliffs and I must have scraped it against a rock. It looks worse than it is.'

'You could have been hurt—'

'Would you care if I was?'

'How can you ask that, Vero?'

His name in her mouth made him lose the ability to breathe, to think, to form a sentence. All he could do was stare and his need for her was so intense, he had to take a breath before he could speak and when he did, his voice shook slightly.

'You know it's indecent how badly I want you. And how many hours I spend thinking about you and what I want to do to you and what I want you to do to me.'

It had been a somewhat circuitous route, but they had got there in the end, and he felt a jolt of triumph and relief because she had finally admitted her desire and now anything was possible. He leaned forward.

'What are you doing?' Her palms flattened against his chest and she pushed him backwards, the slip-sliding intimacy of moments earlier dissolving into her frown and his plunging disappointment.

It had to be addressed. He needed it to be addressed.

'Why are you fighting this?' he said then and

he hated the hoarseness in his voice. Hated it almost as much as he hated the shutters that dropped like guillotines across her eyes. 'Fighting yourself. I know you want it, want me—'

'But that's why it can't happen. Why I have to walk away—'

He stared at her in confusion. He wasn't into being bound or gagged or humiliated. Nor, despite what Betty had said, was he a contrarian. If a woman wasn't interested, he walked away. Or that was what he told himself.

But there was only one woman who had rejected him, and he hadn't walked, he'd been pushed away, only instead of staying away he'd come back for more. Back for her.

And even now when he knew enough to leave well alone, he was still here. And he didn't know what to do with that need to stay. All he knew was that he couldn't fight her and himself at once.

'You're not making any sense.'

'Because you don't understand. You're like everyone else; you see a princess with a crown. Her Most Serene Royal Highness Princess Bettina.' There was a tremor in her voice that shook in time to her hands.

'So, make me understand.'

'I make bad decisions. Stupid choices, the wrong choices and I don't trust myself to make the right ones...'

She didn't finish the sentence. She couldn't. Her hand was pressed over her mouth.

His anger had long since dissolved, but there were other feelings filling the space it had left. Guilt, shock and remorse. He reached out to touch her, but she stumbled backwards.

'No, I don't want you to touch me, I don't want you—'

She wanted him gone, just as she had back in Milan. But this was different. In Milan, she had been angry with him and herself for giving into their desire.

Now there was an ache in her voice. She looked pale, younger, as young as if the last ten years had never happened, and he knew that she was hurt and scared by the pain she was feeling and like an injured animal she wanted to curl up in a ball and hide.

From him.

His chest felt as if it had been ripped open. For so long he had imagined this moment. Imagined seeing Betty crushed, deposed from her throne of complacency and calm. But seeing her in so much distress was unbearable.

'I know.' It hurt more than it should to admit that, but right now his pride was a long way down his list of priorities. 'But I can't leave you like this, so you'll have to make do with me until someone better comes along.'

She burst into tears then and this time when he reached out, she let him pull her close and he held her against him, tight enough that she felt held but not so tight that she couldn't breathe through her tears.

Finally, she let out a shivering breath and, trying not to tense his body, he waited for her to push him away but she just kept leaning into him and, closing his eyes, he brushed his mouth against her hair, breathing in her scent.

Finally, he felt her move and he had to force himself to let go as she inched backwards.

'Do you want me to get Mariangela?'

She shook her head. She still looked pale and gently he pushed her back onto one of the sofas and sat down beside her. 'Here.' He reached into his trousers and pulled out a handkerchief. 'It's clean, I promise.'

He watched her wipe her face. Her lashes were clotted together, and she was still fragile, he realised. But whatever was going on inside her head, it was a burden she needed to shed.

'So what makes you think you can't trust yourself?'

Her head bent low and she didn't reply, and for a moment or two he thought she wasn't going to. But then she took a shaky breath and said, 'I don't think, I know I can't.'

She sounded stubborn, childish almost, but he

sensed that she had been carrying this around with her since childhood. And the tension in her spine suggested she had never told this story to anyone.

'For what reason?'

'Because I killed my mother, and I nearly killed my sister.'

He almost laughed. Whatever he'd been expecting her to say it wasn't that. But then it was so ludicrous. Only looking at her face, he saw that she believed every word.

'That seems unlikely.'

She was shaking her head. 'I told you, I make bad decisions, selfish decisions that end badly. That's why my mother warned me about getting involved with you.'

He frowned. Her mother had warned her? 'I never met your mother.'

'It was the concept of you. For her you were a threat. A scandal in waiting. Her family lost their throne because there were so many scandals and their people got tired of them. It was her biggest fear that would happen in Malaspina. I knew that. I've always known it, and I ignored her. I knew she was worried, but I didn't care. But I didn't realise how much it must have affected her until she had the stroke. And then she kept having them.'

He could hear the guilt in her voice. The regret. Could hear and understand it. He'd had nearly two decades to pick at the guilt and regret and recriminations he felt for getting Tommasino arrested and forgiving himself was still a work in progress.

'You couldn't have known,' he said gently, taking her hand. 'And I doubt your mother would have stopped worrying even if you were the perfect princess.' Reaching out, he tucked a loose strand of hair behind her ear. 'Mothers worry. Mine did, for sure. Even when I towered over her.'

She was shaking her head.

'But I did know about Bella. I knew from when she was little that she had a peanut allergy. And I still let her eat the cake.' The pain in her voice tore through him. Tears were sliding down her face. 'We had to call an ambulance. She could have died. And it was my fault.'

His hand tightened around hers.

'And it must have been terrifying. But you were a kid too and you made a mistake.'

Her mouth was trembling.

'It wasn't a mistake. It was a choice. My parents had some people over for lunch and they brought their children. I wanted to be cool and popular, and everyone was making a fuss of Bella, and I knew if I let her have some cake that she'd go away and for once I'd be the one everyone liked best.'

She pressed her hand against her face again, only not to hold back her tears this time. There was a look of panic in her eyes, as if she had shared something without quite meaning to. Something she was ashamed of revealing.

He stared down at her uncertainly. She looked stricken and he hated seeing her like that. 'You can't think you were responsible. I know you do—' he corrected himself because she so obviously did '—but nobody else would ever think that.'

'But they did.' Her mouth was trembling. 'They thought it and said it.'

'Then I hope your parents had them banished from Malaspina,' he said fiercely.

'No, that didn't happen.' She gave him a small, sad smile that made something inside him crack open. 'Mainly because they were the ones thinking and saying it.'

Vero stared at her in shock. Surely that couldn't be true. But then he thought back to his conversations with the Prince. There had been a chill to the older man's voice when he'd referred to his daughter and the marriage he was setting up for her without her knowledge. At the time he had assumed that Vittorio disliked having to deal directly with someone like Vero. Now though he realised that he had misread the old man and that his haughtiness masked an indifference to his daughter's needs and wishes. That, to him, she was simply an asset to be exploited.

And he had participated in that exploitation.

'They were wrong to do that,' he said, choosing his words carefully. 'But people lash out when they're upset. That isn't what they feel deep down. They know who you are.'

She glanced away and he stared at her profile, the beautiful curve of her cheekbones and the delicate jaw, and he was searching for words when she started speaking.

'Yes, a disappointment.' She breathed out shakily. 'I always have been. My mother's pregnancy with me was difficult. She was horribly ill, and the labour was awful, and of course I wasn't a boy. Even worse, I had the wrong colour hair and freckles, so my father had to endure loads of speculation about that. And I was such a shy and anxious child. Then Bella came along, and they were so different with her. So proud and happy. You know, if Nonno hadn't turned everything upside down I sometimes wonder if they would have asked me to step aside. I tried so hard, I even—' She broke off, frowning.

'Even what?'

'It doesn't matter. None of it matters. Nothing I did, or do, is ever enough.'

Enough. The word scraped across his skin, but he ignored the pain.

'Listen to me, Betty. Whatever you did wrong, however you messed up, that doesn't make you a bad person or a disappointment. You didn't know your mother was ill. As for Bella, you love her and she loves you. But more importantly you take care of her. You look out for her.'

He pulled her against him, wrapping his arms around her, holding her close.

'Everyone messes up. That's how we learn. And young people mess up the most because their brains are wired differently. It's a medically proven fact that they act on impulse and have less ability to self-regulate.' He met her gaze. 'Automotive billionaires have the same problem.'

It was a weak attempt to make her smile and she didn't, but her eyes were soft like smoke. 'Why are you trying to make me feel better? You hate me.'

Had he said that? It felt like a long time ago if he had ever felt it. Stroking her hair, he shook his head. 'I don't hate you. I thought I did. I thought I wanted to punish you. I thought a lot of things apparently.'

He watched her frown, trying to make sense of that last remark, but she was so tired and at that moment a clock chimed the hour and, taking the opportunity to change the subject, he reached out and stroked her face. 'It's late. You need some sleep.'

She let him lead her upstairs like a child, and he waited outside the bathroom as she brushed her teeth and got changed.

'Shall I turn the lamp off?' he asked as she climbed into bed.

She nodded but as she slid down under the sheet, he could feel her reluctance to lose the light. 'Or I could stay for a bit. Until you fall asleep and then I could switch it off,' he said, only realising as he spoke how much he wanted her to agree. How much he wanted to stay, and his dread of having to be separate from her.

'I can't ask you to do that.' She let out a shaky breath.

'You didn't. I offered.'

He sat on the edge of the bed, and after a moment, she reached out and took his hand. 'I do care about you.'

Seconds later she was asleep.

Breathing out unsteadily, he stared down at her, his chest tight, feeling exhausted and relieved. But mostly confused.

Because he had started the evening intending to make Betty admit the truth about her desire for him, to have sex with him not solely for purposes of procreation but pleasure. Only suddenly, even more than he wanted that, he wanted her to trust him. To trust herself. If he could do that then maybe the two of them could...

Could what?

The answer to that question kept him sitting on her bed until, exasperated by the complexity of his feelings, he let go of Betty's hand and went to sit on the sofa, where it stayed unanswered because he found that he had another, more pressing question.

Surely her first husband was the one person who liked her best. Why then hadn't she told Alberto what she had just told him?

CHAPTER EIGHT

BETTY WOKE UP with a start.

She had been dreaming. Of Vero. They were in her grandfather's little green sports car, driving in the hills behind Morroello. There were no landmarks, but she recognised the road, and she was driving, and Vero was smiling that megawatt smile that made her bones soften and her breath turn to air.

And then the road took a sudden, unexpected turn to the right and suddenly they were heading towards a cliff edge and Vero was undoing his seat belt and getting to his feet and for a moment he stood there, poised and calm, and then he was gone, and the car was tipping forward and she was falling, falling—

Breathing out shakily, she pulled the sheet around her.

Last night she had opened up to Vero in a way that she had never done with anyone.

Bella knew, and her nanny had known, but behaved as if she hadn't. Outside that, it was only Nonno who had, somewhat surprisingly, guessed at her parents' cruelty and manipulation. But was that surprising? For all his careless, rakish ways, her grandfather was astute and observant. A people person, unlike her parents.

Their disappointment in her was painful enough to live with in private. Discussing it with other people would simply add to the shame. Worst-case scenario, they might even take her parents' point of view. After all, the facts were clear and undeniable. That in her desperation for approval she had put both her mother's and sister's health at risk.

It was why she had worked so hard to be the perfect princess. That fear of exposure and the potential for yet more humiliation and pain.

And yet she had chosen to confide in Vero. She still didn't know why she had opened up to him. It made no sense. He hated her. Saw only the bad in her. And not in some abstract way. He was back in her life because he'd wanted to punish her for what she had said to him all those years ago, for how she had made him feel and for what her father had done to his family.

Rolling onto her side, she stared across the room to where Vero lay sprawled on the sofa, still dressed, his feet hanging over the arm, his head wedged uncomfortably up against one of the large, embroidered cushions.

She stared at his sculpted face, her heart skipping forward.

Last night she had not just let her mask slip but smashed it to pieces. She had shown him her scars, letting him see the frailest, ugliest part of herself. She had been his to hurt.

But he hadn't hurt her. Despite having motive, means and opportunity he had listened and comforted and cared enough that it felt like love.

No, she thought firmly. Not again.

Because what did she know about love? The romantic kind anyway.

Her parents' marriage had been a masterclass of pragmatism on both sides. There was understanding and affection of sorts. And she had recreated that with Alberto.

Minus the understanding and affection.

With Vero she had thought she was in love. Thought he was in love with her, but in truth their relationship had largely been a sexual one. A sexual awakening for her, and perhaps for him too, she thought, remembering those afternoons on his bed, his hands trembling, white-knuckled against the sheets, as she took him in her mouth.

But as she'd since found out, you didn't need to love someone or trust them or even respect them to have good sex.

At the time though, in her naivety, she had conflated sex with love and lust with that consummation of a need that went beyond the physicality of bodies and breath. And she had been a willing participant. Eager, in fact. And she could admit now that if Vero hadn't said what he had, she would have given up everything for him. Because it was better to have someone pretend to be in love with you than nobody loving you for real.

And now?

She tensed as Vero shifted in his sleep, rearranging his limbs and rolling onto his side so that if his eyes had been open, they would have been looking straight at one another.

He had done more than look. Last night, he had seen past the facade, seen who she really was, and he hadn't moved away, hadn't pushed her away. He had held her and stroked her hair and made space for her between his arms.

Which was kind and compassionate, and compassion was a form of love. But it was the kind you might offer to children and injured animals. In short, it was simply part of a universal humanity that made people bond and look out for each other.

And her best chance of making this marriage 'work' was to remember that, and not get distracted by the way his eyes seemed to soak her up.

The following morning, she woke late, later than she had done in years.

Someone had opened the shutters a fraction,

just enough to let in the cooler, morning air. Even before she glanced at the clock, she could tell from the intensity of the light that dawn was a distant memory. For a moment, she stared at the view through the window, taking pleasure in the strip of blue sky and sea, and then everything from the night before rolled over her like a wave and she sat up.

Vero.

But aside from the cushions sitting plumply at either end, the sofa was empty. She felt his absence sting her skin, but had she really expected him to wait for her to wake up?

Unsurprisingly, given that it was nearly half past ten, there was no sign of Vero at the breakfast table, and, stemming her disappointment, she nibbled a pastry and drank some black coffee before wandering oh-so-casually through the sitting room and onto the terrace.

But Vero wasn't there either. Nor was he by the pool or in the orchard or on the beach. Back at the house, she dithered about asking Mariangela but just as she was crunching her way across the gravel, she noticed that the door to the garage was ajar.

Pushing it wider, she stepped inside, her pulse skipping a beat as she breathed in the familiar scent of warm leather and oil. It took a minute for her eyes to adjust to the gloom. Her grandfather's pistachio-coloured convertible was sitting where it always did. Glancing at it, she stiffened. Usually it was covered, but someone had taken the soft top off.

'This is one dope whip, Princess.'

She felt a jolt of heat as Vero stepped out of the shadows, moving in that loose-limbed way of his that made her skin tingle and, gazing into the half-light, she almost lost her balance.

He was wearing a black T-shirt that stretched endlessly across his shoulders and slouchy blue jeans and with his dark hair falling in front of his eyes and the light striping across his face it was like tumbling back in time.

'Two questions. One, when were you going to tell me that there was a 1955 Alfa Romeo Giulietta Spider on the premises?' he said, walking slowly alongside the car, his fingers trailing, almost caressing the glossy paintwork. 'Secondly, why is that big, ugly behemoth out on the drive instead of this little beauty?'

'By "big, ugly behemoth", I take it you mean the limo?' She met his gaze. 'That's my official car. My father prefers me to use that for security reasons.'

He held her eyes for a split second. 'What a waste. So who drives it? Please tell me it's not Mariangela. I saw her trying to put some roasting tins in the oven yesterday and I'm not going to lie, she has no spatial awareness.'

There was a moment of silence as their eyes met. Quickly, in case she saw pity there, she gave him a small, tight smile and said, 'Thank you for yesterday. For mopping me up and listening. I'm sorry for burdening you with all that.'

He smiled, one of those curling, 'raised by loving parents and never had to question his own worth' smiles that made her breath feel hot in her throat. 'That's what a husband is supposed to do, isn't it?'

Yes, it was.

But Alberto had shown no interest in the inner workings of her mind. He had shared her parents' attitude that an aristocratic marriage worked best as a union whose purpose was to cement an alliance or shared wealth.

She took a steadying breath. It was uncomfortable thinking about Alberto when Vero was standing so close. Like a betrayal. Only not of Alberto but of Vero. It was the same feeling she'd had when her father had told her that he had found a suitor for her just a week after she and Vero had broken up.

It had felt wrong then. It still felt wrong now. But there was a way to make it right.

'There's something I need to tell you. I wanted

to tell you before, right after it happened, but obviously that wasn't possible.

'I wanted you to know that Alberto wasn't waiting in the wings. And I wasn't waiting for a prince. I know what it must have looked like, but I never met Alberto until the day our engagement was announced.'

Vero's deep green eyes didn't so much as blink, but she could feel him processing her words.

'Why did you marry him so soon after we split, then?'

'After you, after we— My mother thought I needed to be settled. And my parents wanted the match.'

'Did they force you?'

She hadn't needed forcing. She had been numb. Uncaring. But then her parents had known that.

'My mother had had the first stroke and my father blamed me. It felt like the least I could do. And everyone wanted it to happen.'

'And what did you want?'

You, she thought. And she had admitted so much already, but that was too much.

'I wanted to please them. And they were worried somebody would find out I'd slept with you, and Alberto didn't care that I wasn't a virgin. That's why it all happened so quickly.'

'And then he died.'

'Yes.' She breathed out shakily. 'But I didn't want him to die. I might not have loved Alberto, but I never wanted that.'

He pulled her closer. 'Of course not.' His face creased. 'I thought you wanted to marry him. If I'd known that you had no choice... I just wish I'd been there to stand up for you.'

'I thought you wanted to punish me,' she said slowly. 'Not take on my father.'

'I did but I've ended up punishing myself instead.'

She stared up at Vero in confusion, but he was looking back at the car. 'You never said who gets to drive it.'

'No one at the moment. It can't be driven. The cam belt is busted. I ordered a new one but it's such a long time since I looked at an engine and I was nervous about handing her over to just anyone. How did you get in here?' she added, glancing over at the door. 'Wasn't it locked?'

'Yes, Nancy Drew, it was. But I'm on good terms with the owner. Or I think I could be,' he said then. 'If she'd give me a chance. Or it might even be a second chance.'

He took another step forward and stopped in front of her.

Her breath hitched. She knew that it was risky to stand that close to him. Knew too that it was the leather and oil smell acting like catnip on her senses but any input from her frontal lobe had got lost somewhere between the sweet, eager look on his face and the snatch of her breath.

'And what would you do with this second chance?' she said slowly.

In the soft sunlight filtering in through the half-open door, his skin was smooth and even and his green eyes were serious and steady.

'Look, I know all of this is fake. But I think we've been focusing so much on what's fake, we've forgotten what's real. So why don't we just forget about the wedding and the honeymoon and have some fun being plain old Betty and Vero? Do you think we could do that? Would you like to do that?'

Her heart, which had been beating steadily until then, began to race. It was the first time that Vero had asked for her opinion, her assent, since he'd walked into the Prince's Palace all those weeks ago.

The first time she could remember anyone asking for her opinion or assent in probably her whole life.

Maybe it was that fact or perhaps it was how he was looking at her as if nothing else existed in the world, but she found herself nodding. 'How would that work?'

A tension she hadn't realised was there seemed

to ease from his shoulders and jaw and she watched mesmerised as the sunlight licked a path along the curve of his cheekbone.

'I had my yacht brought to the island this morning.'

He had? She stared at him dazedly.

'It was only a short hop from Capri.' The shrug that accompanied that statement transformed him from the son of the chauffeur into an automotive billionaire whose every wish became reality with the sending of a text. 'She's moored at the jetty. I thought we could take her out and go do some diving. You can snorkel, can't you?'

She nodded again. 'I haven't done it in a while.'

'But you enjoy it?'

She almost nodded again but caught herself at the last moment. 'Yes.'

'Then let's go do it.'

Was that it? She'd asked herself the same question when her father had agreed to her not marrying Vero. But then she'd felt as if she were standing on a trapdoor that was going to suddenly open beneath her feet.

This felt different. Easy. Effortless. Just as it used to, and she stared up at him dizzily. They were standing close enough that she could have reached out and touched those miraculous cheekbones and it was impossible not to focus on their closeness.

Clearing her throat, she said quickly, 'I'll go and tell Mariangela.'

An hour later she was swimming through the clear, cool water of the Tyrrhenian Sea.

Gianluca, the yacht's captain, had dropped anchor near the Cala Gaetano, a secluded crescent-shaped cove where the water was closer to green than blue.

The beach itself was covered in stones but the reason for stopping lay beneath the waves several metres from the shore, as Betty discovered when she submerged her head and shoulders. Instantly all sounds were muted and the sun and the sky were forgotten. It was like being in another, hidden world. There was so much to see that wasn't visible from the surface. Octopus and crabs and tiny, dancing seahorses. And it was easy to forget all those land-based expectations that normally followed her like a shadow.

'We'll have to wait a bit before we go back in,' Vero said as they sat down for lunch. 'I wouldn't want you to get cramps.'

She nodded. 'I'm happy to wait.'

Not just happy to wait, she thought with a jolt. Just happy, and lighter, as if a burden had been lifted. But then it had. Talking to Vero, unpicking her past with him, unpicking their past, had been uncomfortable but holding everything in had been breaking her from the inside out.

She hadn't planned on telling him anything. Quite the opposite in fact. It was humbling enough to admit that her parents viewed her primarily as a puppet on a string. Revealing that out loud, and to the man who had shared their opinion, would be an act of deliberate and unnecessary self-harm. Like rubbing salt into a wound.

Her eyes moved to his face, to the impossible symmetry of his features.

But Vero had been not salt, but a salve. He had listened, and offered not pity but comfort. He had made her realise that the House of Marchetta was a house of mirrors, each one reflecting a different, distorting view. Looking into his green eyes, she had seen herself as he saw her, not as a disappointment or an idealised, perfect princess, but as Betty.

'Or we could go looking for dolphins.' Vero had looked up from his food and was gazing at her across the table. 'Gianluca says he saw a school off Santo Stefano.'

'I'd love that,' she said truthfully, and then because she wanted to, and because now it was easy to do so, she added, 'And maybe tomorrow we could go and see the cathedral cliffs at Palmarola.'

It wasn't storming the barricades, but it felt undeniably good to say what *she* wanted to do.

'Sounds like a plan.' Vero held her gaze. 'Maybe we should renew our wedding vows while we're there. Just the two of us.'

His words oscillated between them in the bright sunshine. But that was all they were, she reminded herself. Just words that happened to be spoken by an intensely beautiful man who was also the only man she'd ever loved.

The dolphins didn't disappoint. She had seen them before when she had gone out with Alberto as part of the official engagement photo shoot but, in truth, she could hardly remember their marriage, much less one isolated day.

Vero's deceit and his absence had undone her, turned her world dark and she had been alone in the darkness. Who could she have talked to about her broken heart? Not her parents. Not Bella, who had still been a child. And not her husband.

And then first her mother, then Alberto, had died. One after the other, and there had been more pain and guilt and regret. In the everlasting, formless grey of her life, she had learned to live through Bella and all the colours of her younger sister's hopes and dreams.

But today she was here, on a yacht, breathing in fresh sea air, feeling restless and hopeful and planning for tomorrow. And it was because of Vero.

She glanced over to where he was leaning against the rail. 'Thank you for today.'

'My pleasure.'

The word pressed inside her head like a stone inside a boot.

They had touched so many times yesterday and today in a completely non-sexual way but now she felt almost shy around him. And he was being careful too. At one point she had lost her balance and he'd caught her arm to steady her and she had felt his touch like a current of electricity. But then he'd immediately let go when she'd found her footing. As if he'd burned his fingers.

Or was scared of what he might do if he didn't let go.

'Do you want to go and get changed?' His eyes lingered on hers, then shifted away to the rippling blue water. He looked as if he wanted to dive in. To her, not the water.

They hadn't talked about sex since that explosive conversation in her bedroom but there was no need. It was always there. Blooming and charging the air around them like a heat shimmer above the roads that criss-crossed the Malaspinian countryside, changing the way they looked at one another and how they breathed and moved.

She glanced down at herself. She was wearing one of Vero's shirts over a bikini. 'It's fine. I'll change when we get back to the villa.'

'You could. If we were going back to the villa.'

'Are we not?'

Shaking his head, he took a step closer then and she felt the usual current of heat snake between them as he reached out and caught her lightly by the wrists, and his voice was low and a little scratchy as he said, 'We will later. But first, you and I are going to have some fun in Rome.'

Betty had been to Rome multiple times. Most recently she had accompanied her father to a dinner with various European trade delegations. But she had never been solely for fun.

But then she hardly went anywhere solely for fun. The odd day out with Bella, the occasional weekend in Ponza. And she had never been anywhere with Vero.

Their relationship had been a series of covert encounters, some little more than feverish embraces.

Now she was sitting in a taxi, holding Vero's hand as the driver manoeuvred through Rome's traffic.

'We could have gone back to the villa. I have a wardrobe of dresses and event wear.'

'Princess Bettina goes to events. You're Betty,

remember? And Betty doesn't wear formal gowns and tiaras. So, first things first, you're going to choose something to wear tonight and then we're going to go to my apartment to get changed.'

'You have an apartment?'

'*Sì.*' He nodded. 'I use it when I'm in the area.'

'In the area? Are you talking about Italy or Europe?'

His mouth curved up fractionally and as usual she forgot to breathe when he smiled.

'Italy. I have another apartment in Paris and a house in London. I travel a lot and I'm not a fan of hotels. Too little control. Too many interruptions,' he added obliquely. 'Here's fine,' he said, switching to Italian as he caught the driver's eye.

'Okay, the rule is, there are no rules,' he said as he helped Betty out of the taxi. Leaning in, he kissed her softly on the mouth. 'Pick anything. But promise me that it's what the real Betty would choose.'

That was a promise worth making, he thought two hours later as Betty walked into the huge, open-plan sitting room in his apartment wearing faded jeans and—

His breath punched in his throat.

That was some top.

His eyes moved hungrily to the oscillating

cowl of fabric that almost reached her waist. Or more accurately to the occasional glimpse of smooth, bare skin it offered whenever she moved.

It was casual and punch-in-the-gut sexy, and she looked completely different from the poised, demure princess known to the world. And yet to him, she had never looked more like herself.

Breathing out unevenly, he felt his gaze move to her hair.

Naturally it fell into soft waves, which Betty almost always contained and controlled and smoothed into a bun. But now it hung loose, the mass of autumn-coloured curls tumbling past her shoulders and fanning out riotously around her face, part Pre-Raphaelite, part flower child.

In the past when she was with him, she hardly ever wore it down.

Except in bed.

He sucked in a breath, remembering the weight of it in his hands and how he could twist it into a kind of rope.

'Hi,' she said quietly.

His head was spinning.

If this was the real Betty, then he wanted to do more than say 'hi'. A whole lot more. Tamping down the pornographic slideshow in his head, he walked over and stopped in front of her.

'You look—you look incredible.'

She was nervous, he could tell. 'Do you think?'

What he thought was that he would be spending the evening staring down his rivals like some primate marking his territory. What he thought was that he had a whole day planned and she had just made it a thousand times harder for him to stick to that plan. But this wasn't about him.

It was about Betty.

It was about giving her the freedom and fun her life had lacked.

His chest felt tight. He was still stunned by what she had told him.

Hearing her talk about how her parents had treated her made him want to smash things with his bare hands. It seemed impossible. How could it not? Betty was a princess. To the rest of the world, she lived a charmed, cosseted life behind the palace walls. But behind those walls she had been manipulated and gaslit, been judged and found wanting by the very people who should have been protecting and praising her.

Including him.

He hated himself for that. It was bad enough that he hadn't seen or chosen to see what was happening in front of him. Instead, he had made assumptions. Seen her serenity as evidence of a power she didn't have.

But worse still, he had been complicit. Her parents might have manipulated her into her first marriage, but he had played a part in forcing her into the second.

'Can a goddess be too much?' he said, pulling her closer so that he could have counted all her beautiful freckles if she'd asked him to.

She smiled. 'I'm a princess not a goddess.'

'You are definitely a goddess, *dolcezza*. Right. Let's go. *Andiamo.*'

And, grabbing her hand, he towed her towards the lift before he did something stupid like sliding his hands under that shimmering, shifting top.

CHAPTER NINE

THEY ATE AT Il Pellicano, a trattoria that served unpretentious Roman dishes to in-the-know locals rather than tourists. It was busy and buzzing and they ate at the counter, pausing to talk and occasionally offer each other a mouthful of their food.

Which was something he'd never done before and wouldn't do again with Betty, not in public anyway, he thought, his pulse stumbling as he watched her lips close around the mouthful of the risotto he'd ordered.

After dinner, they walked through the streets, holding hands. It was strange. Handholding was such an innocuous gesture and yet it felt radical to feel her fingers clasping his in full view of everyone. Not that everyone was looking at them.

Some people looked.

As he'd predicted, Betty was the subject of a lot of, admittedly furtive, male gazes but nobody did anything more than glance.

'Do you think anyone has recognised us?'

Hearing the anxiety in her voice, he shook his head. 'How could they? Nobody knows Betty and Vero here.'

She tried to smile but there were two little frown lines on her forehead and he pressed his thumb against them to smooth them flat. 'Nobody is looking for us so they won't see us. Even if they do look, you don't look like Princess Bettina and I'm just some anonymous guy nobody cares about.'

'You're not anonymous. People all over the world drive your cars. You're a household name. And people do care about you. Your family, your friends, your staff.' She hesitated. 'I care about you, remember?'

They had reached the nightclub, but he barely noticed, he was too lost in the simplicity and truth of her words.

'I care about you too.'

They stared at one another, silent and unmoving like rocks in a river as people surged round them. 'Are we going in?' Betty said finally.

He nodded. 'Yeah, let's do that.'

The club was rammed.

'Can we do shots?' she asked as they reached the bar.

Frankly, he already felt somewhat intoxicated by her nearness and that oscillating tease of a drop but this was Betty's night.

'Here.' He handed her the shot glass. Betty drank hers and then took his hand and turned towards the dance floor.

'You want to dance now?'

Beneath the strobe lights, her eyes were darker than shadows. 'I've wanted to dance with you for ever.'

'We danced at the wedding.'

'Not like that. Not some waltz with everyone watching. I want to dance like we did at the palace that time.'

The expression on her face was so soft, so open, he forgot to speak. 'I want that too,' he said after a moment, and he let her lead him onto the dance floor.

This was a different kind of dancing from the wedding waltz. For starters the dance floor was full of people pressed up close to one another and nobody was looking at anyone. A lot of them had their eyes shut and were just weaving to the bassline. The room radiated heat and sweat and freedom.

And he felt freer than he'd ever felt. As free as Betty looked, turning in the circle of his arms, her own arms reaching above her head. Free to look at her openly, to lean in and breathe in her scent and let it settle in his brain. Free to touch her waist, to press his hand against the warm damp skin of her back.

'Are you having fun?'

Her eyes rested on his face and she nodded and then she looped her arms around his neck.

'Yes.' She laughed against his mouth and kissed him and the floor tilted sideways. Or maybe that was him because everyone else kept dancing. And he told himself to get a grip but that only made his hand press her closer.

She moaned softly and the sound made him feel light-headed and powerful and enslaved. Was that what she wanted? It was what he wanted. But not here. With an effort of will, he broke the kiss.

There was an empty booth at the edge of the dance floor and he shouldered his way through the sticky mass of dancers. 'Do you want another drink?'

'I could get them.'

He hesitated. 'I don't know if that's the best idea.'

'It's what Betty would do.'

His eyes jerked up to that bee-stung mouth like a compass needle finding its magnetic north. He wanted to beg her forgiveness. He wanted to lick into her mouth and between her thighs until she was begging him to do anything he wanted.

He watched her make her way to the bar. Watched the barman's eyes widen appreciatively. His own eyes narrowed but Betty was already returning, only without the drinks. She was no longer smiling. Instead, she looked tense and anxious.

'What is it? What happened? Did the barman say something to you?'

'No.' She glanced over her shoulder. 'I just saw Edoardo and Cicciu. I don't think they recognised me—'

'Who are they?'

'Their father is the Duca di Monte Giusto. He's a friend of my father. He and his wife came to the wedding. You probably don't remember them.'

Vero felt as though his chest were being pushed through a shredder. He knew his face must be showing his shock and that it must be obvious to Betty. Any minute now she would notice and ask him what was wrong.

'How well do you know them?'

He had spoken more harshly than he'd intended and she glanced up at him, her eyes widening. 'Well enough.' She bit into her lip. 'I think we should go.'

By 'go' she meant run.

'Why should we leave because of them?' They were his family. His half-brothers. It made his head spin even just thinking that sentence inside his head. Not only the sudden, shocking truth of it but the fact that to them it wasn't a truth. To them, he was just a random man in a nightclub. That even if they met and he was introduced, there would be no nod of recognition. He had no doubt whatsoever that the Duke would have kept his existence a secret from them and suddenly he was fifteen again, and feeling an anger that seemed to lift him off his feet and smack him to the ground because Betty was doing exactly what his father had done, what her father had done. She couldn't deny his existence or evict him, but she wanted to sweep him away.

And he had given her the power to do so.

She blinked. 'Because if they see us then they'll make a scene.'

'I thought you wanted to be yourself.'

'I do...'

Someone who wasn't so attuned to Betty's every breath might have missed the infinitesimal flinch that accompanied her response, but Vero saw it, and heard the slight hitch to her breath that accompanied it.

He was being unfair, cruel even, expecting Betty to face her fear when he couldn't even say his out loud, but adrenaline was soaring through his body. He could taste it in his mouth, and he hated that it came from fear and shame. Hated that he could use so many words to not say what needed to be said.

'Then why are you running and hiding? Your

father isn't here. I am. But that doesn't count for anything, does it, Betty? Because you never forget, not even for one night, that you're a princess.'

'Why are you being like this? What are you doing?'

He had got to his feet. 'You wanted to go. So, let's go.'

The journey back to the villa was silent. He couldn't find the right words, any words in fact, that could explain why he had acted as he had. And maybe Betty too was lost for words.

Lost to him.

As they walked back into the villa, she stopped and turned to him.

'I know you're upset that I wanted to leave. But that can't be the only reason.'

'Oh, because it couldn't be you. So, I guess it has to be me. So why don't you just say what you're thinking, which is that I'm the problem?'

'That's not what I'm thinking. I just think there must be something else, only I don't know what it is. And I can't help you if—'

'Help me.' He felt his jaw clench. 'You've never helped me. In fact, you made things worse. You saw who I was and made me believe that I was good enough. And just for a short time, you wanted what I wanted. But you couldn't do it, could you? You couldn't follow through. Just like tonight, you bottled it.'

He could see her shock, her pain, but he had smashed everything to pieces, so many pieces and he didn't know how to fix what he'd done and so he stood and watched her turn and walk up the stairs, and then a moment later, he heard the soft click of her bedroom door, and he turned too.

Closing the door, Betty felt her legs give way and, breathing out unevenly, she slid down to the floor. She felt sick, winded, shivery with shock. Vero was like a stranger. An angry, green-eyed stranger. And she felt as if she were living in a nightmare, only there was no way out because she was already awake.

And it hurt, hearing the hostility in his voice and seeing that distance in his eyes as if he didn't know her. As if she hadn't spent the last twenty-four hours peeling away her armour.

Her legs were shaking now and she hugged them against her chest, trying to hold them steady.

She had been so happy earlier, happy to be herself and to be with Vero.

Only something had happened.

She pictured Vero's face at the club. He had been anxious about her, concerned, and that had been so sweet of him, only then she had told him who she'd seen at the bar and he had flipped. But

that didn't make any sense. He'd never even met
Edoardo and Cicciu.

Perhaps he just hated dancing. After all, it was
the second time he'd virtually dragged her away
from a dance floor.

She had a sudden, sharp memory of the moment when Vero had bumped into the Duca di
Monte Giusto. There had been no acknowledge-
ment there, which was odd in itself, particularly
as it had felt as if something had passed between
the two men.

Then suddenly they had been leaving. At the
time it had all happened so quickly, and she had
been furious with Vero, mainly because she had
known that once they left the party, they would
be alone together.

Now, though, she could remember more, remember how he had been tense in exactly the
same way. Like a sail stretched taut in a running wind.

And he was taut now. Angry too, almost like
someone in shock.

Her legs had stopped shaking and she got unsteadily to her feet. She kicked off her towering
heels and considered finding her flip-flops but
then she turned and opened the door because
when someone needed your help, every second
counted. And Vero needed her help.

She walked swiftly downstairs, moving

through the villa. There was no sign of him anywhere, but she knew where he was almost as if he'd left a trail of pebbles for her.

The garage door was open. Slipping inside, she stopped, her bare feet pressing into the cool concrete floor.

Nonno's car sat in a shaft of moonlight looking exactly as it had yesterday. Except that Vero was sitting behind the wheel.

His head was lowered, and he didn't look up as she approached, not even when she opened the door and sat down in the passenger seat.

They sat in silence for what felt like a long time, but she waited because she knew how hard it was to admit something painful to oneself. To admit it to someone else was like consciously turning a car round and driving straight into a hurricane. It required a different level of courage and steadiness and only the driver could choose when to turn the steering wheel and press down hard on the accelerator pedal.

'When I was fifteen,' he said then, 'my dad lost his job. He was working at a garage, repairing cars, and the owner sold the site to a developer, and we had to move house. We couldn't afford to pay anyone to help so me and my dad did all the moving with some help from the neighbours. My mum had this chest of drawers that she had by her bed and somehow it got put in my room.'

Now he lifted his head.

'I wasn't prying. I had to take the drawers out so that I could lift it. That's when I found the envelope. It had my name on it. That's why I opened it.'

She felt oddly calm even though her heart was racing.

'What was in it?'

His face, his beautiful, fine features were as unreadable as bronze and she was trying to think of something eloquent that might unlock him when he said, 'My birth certificate. It was tough at home. There was never that much money. My mum was only eighteen when she had me and I blamed my dad for not being more careful. For a long time, I gave him a hard time. Except it turned out he wasn't to blame because he's not my dad, biologically anyway.'

'The Duke,' she said softly.

He turned, his green eyes jagged looking like bits of broken glass. 'You knew?'

'No.' She shook her head. 'Not until I went upstairs a moment ago. And I didn't know. I just remembered when we were dancing—'

Vero's mouth twisted. 'Yeah, he wasn't pleased to see me. But then he wasn't pleased the first time we met either.'

'He asked to meet you?'

He shook his head and there was something in that small movement that tore her up inside.

'I had a temper then. He has one too. It's probably the one thing he's ever given me. When I found the birth certificate, I had a huge row with my mum and then I went over to his house. I thought—I don't know what I thought,' he admitted after a moment.

Young people act on impulse, she thought.

'I guess I thought he might be curious about me. Curious to meet his own flesh and blood. But he wasn't curious. He was furious. He thought I was looking for money...' His voice slowed as the sentence fizzled out.

'So, he'd had an affair with your mum. But he must have had the boys by then.'

Vero nodded. 'She was their au pair.'

Betty was stunned. Horrified. 'Did anyone know?'

Vero shrugged. 'I don't think so. It wasn't serious, for him anyway. But he was rich, and he bought her nice things, and he told her that he loved her. And then she told him she was pregnant, and he ended it. He sacked her. She never saw him again. He never got in touch. He didn't even know that I was a boy. He washed his hands of her and me.'

Betty felt sick. No wonder Vero had been so angry with her. The Duke had got rid of his mother to punish her for getting pregnant, and then history had basically repeated itself when her father had sacked Tommasino, knowing instinctively that would be the most effective way to punish Vero.

'What did you say to him?'

'I was pretty out of shape. I shouted at him and then this maid came into the room and said my dad was there and the Duke said that Tommasino had been paid already. That he'd signed a legally binding contract to marry my mum and take me on and that there would be no more money.'

'He paid Tommasino to do that?'

'It probably felt like a lot at the time because neither of them had any money, but it wasn't. That was hard. Finding out how little I was worth. But also, I felt so guilty. You know, I'd been giving my dad grief for years for getting my mum pregnant and he never rose to it.' His voice sounded taut as if he was having to keep control. 'He never put me right. He took it because he wanted to protect me.'

'He's a good man,' Betty said quietly. 'And so are you.' Reaching out, she touched Vero's hand.

'No, I'm not. I lost my temper and then the Duke did too, and my dad tried to calm things and somehow the Duke got knocked down and he cut his hand and then he called some mate of his at the police and they came and cuffed my dad. And that's when the Duke told me that he would let Tommasino off but that it would go on his record and if I bothered him again then my dad would be arrested again.'

He looked devastated. 'So, I'm not a good man. My mum was petrified the whole time that I wouldn't be able to keep away. And my dad had this threat hanging over him. Because of me.'

'No, not because of you. Because of a situation over which you had no control. You can't blame yourself, Vero. You were fifteen years old.'

'Maybe, but I can blame myself for this. Your father is partly to blame but I am too. I forced you into this marriage. I just wanted to prove to the Duke that he was wrong. That I wasn't disposable, that I was worthy. And I knew if I married you that I would have a title because your father would insist on it and then I would be equal to him, and he'd have to acknowledge me.'

She could hear the pain of his teenage self pushing through the words and the newer pain layered on top.

'I know. I knew that nine years ago.'

There was a shifting silence.

'What do you mean?' He frowned. 'I didn't want you for your title nine years ago.'

Now she frowned. 'But you told me that's what you wanted. We talked about getting serious and—'

'And I said, "Are we talking about marriage?"'
Vero held her gaze. 'And you said, "What would
you say if I was?"'

'And you said, "Yes, obviously. Who doesn't
want to marry a princess?"' she said, the words
as crushing now as they had been then.

He nodded, his throat working through a swallow, and she felt his fingers curl around hers.
'Because I thought you were joking, and then
you said you were. You said that you wouldn't
marry the son of a chauffeur. That you were a
princess, and you would marry a prince. And
then you did.'

She could feel her pulse beating heavily. Vero
was staring at her. They were a foot apart, close
enough that she could see the truth in his eyes,
touch it almost.

'I only said that to hurt you because you hurt
me.' She pressed her hand against her forehead.
'I kept hearing what my mother said about you.
That I shouldn't get too close to you. That I was
being naive, and then you said that thing about
princesses—'

And she had panicked. Pain and anger had
followed but in that moment all she'd felt was
a swirling fear. Because she'd known what it
meant. Known that it had to end.

So that was what she had done. Only it hadn't
needed to end.

She felt a terrible sadness then at the pointless-ness of it all. 'I hurt you for no reason.'

'We both hurt each other.' In the moonlight, his eyes on hers were wide and unflinching. 'But I'm the one who came back to hurt you some more.'

'You were angry—'

'Don't do that.' His anger was abrupt and in-tense. 'Don't minimise your feelings at the ex-pense of mine or anyone else's. You matter, Betty. And I made you unhappy.'

'I know, but I made you unhappy too, and admitting it doesn't change that. And it doesn't make me weak. It makes me honest, and I want us to be honest.'

He took a fast breath. 'I want that too.'

'Good.' She felt that shared desire for some-thing other than sex press softly around her. 'That's good because everything bad that's hap-pened to us happened because of lies and I don't want to lie any more. So yes, you made me un-happy, but today you made me happy. Happier than I've ever been.'

He was staring at her, scanning her face, and there was a fine tremor in his voice as he said, 'Do you mean that?'

How could she not be happy? She was in love. Hopelessly and completely in love. And it was as terrifying as it was beautiful. And she wanted to tell him the truth; it was what she said she'd wanted. But he was vulnerable right now, and love had failed him in the past. Maybe it would be better to give him some breathing space.

She nodded. 'It's a low bar, but yes.' She was still trying to smile when he pulled her closer, wrapping his arms around her, and she felt his heart slow to a steady, hypnotic rhythm.

'I wanted to hurt you too. That's why I said that thing about not having sex unless I was ovulating. But I didn't mean it. Or maybe I did at the time, but I don't mean it now.'

She felt every cell in his body tense. Even the air stilled and the silence around them felt loaded.

He shifted against her, inching back just far enough that their eyes were level, and then he reached out and ran his finger down the side of her face. It was the lightest of touches, a whisper of a caress but she felt it ripple through her like an electromagnetic pulse.

He stared at her for one long, swelling moment.

'Are you saying…?'

'Yes,' she said hoarsely.

The kiss that came after was hot and slow and sweet and inexorable. As he parted her lips, she moaned against his mouth, her body softening, stirring.

They'd had sex in the garage in the past but

never in any of the cars so it felt both familiar and new.

'Are you sure?'

She pressed her hand against his already hard erection, and he grunted low in his throat as he shifted the seat as far back as it would go and lifted her over the gearstick and onto his lap.

'Help me undress,' she whispered.

Vero breathed out unevenly, her words acting like gasoline on a bonfire. He tugged at the buttons of her jeans and then pulled them down her thighs and over her bare feet, taking her panties with them. Sliding his hand between her legs, he felt how wet she was, and his breath swelled in his throat.

She moaned as he slid his fingers inside her, and then he reached under that top, that maddening tease of a top, and found her breasts.

Her nipples were hard, and she made that sound he liked as he pinched them gently, then a little harder, watching her eyes grow glassy with a need that matched his own.

'I want to touch you,' she said hoarsely and he watched mesmerised as she unbuttoned his trousers and then her hand was closing around the hard, smooth length of him and, gripping her waist, he breathed out, breathed in the feeling of her thumb and fingers circling him, slipping back and forth until he had to dig his heels into the footwell of the car to stop himself lifting up his pelvis and ending things too quickly.

Batting her hands away, he lifted her up. He cupped her bottom in his hands and leaned her back against the steering wheel, moulding her pliant flesh with his fingers before dipping his face between her thighs.

He loved this. Loved the taste of her and the way her breath hitched when he licked her. She was already close and then her thighs tightened around his head, and she let out a small, hoarse cry. Then she arched against his mouth, and he felt her body contracting and expanding in long, expansive shudders as he felt her pleasure everywhere.

'Can you go behind me?' she murmured as he lowered her back into his lap and, nodding wordlessly, he helped her lean over the seat and then positioned himself behind her naked bottom, bracing himself against the frame of the door, his pulse accelerating as she tilted her pelvis up slightly and he pushed inside her, moving slowly at first then deepening his thrusts until he could feel her pressed up tight against him.

He'd been going to hold back but then he felt her fingers slide up his thigh to cradle him in her hand and suddenly everything, his breath, his body, his hunger, was beyond his ability to control, and he was in freefall. And then his orgasm tore through him, and he wrapped his arms around her stomach and ground into her until his body shook.

Vero woke to find Betty curled against him, her arm flung across his chest, her breath warm against his throat. Shifting slightly, he eased backwards just enough that he could watch her sleep. They had made it upstairs to Betty's bedroom and he had stripped her first and then himself. Yes, having sex in the car had been unbound and exhilarating, but the bed had more scope for his and her imaginations.

He had let her take charge. Let her guide him to where she wanted to be touched and stroked and licked and held, keeping himself in check. Over and over and over again until it got too intense, and she pushed his head or his hand away.

And then he waited, his thumbs grazing her nipples, his tongue tracing circles on her skin until she reached for him again.

He still couldn't get his head around it. But it had happened. The world was rearranging itself so that he no longer had to fantasise about having Betty in his arms or splayed out under his surging body. He didn't have to conjure up memories of her sweet, serious face on his pillow. Or wake in the morning and have to discover that her presence was simply a dream.

Now he could reach out as his eyes opened
and know that she would be there beside him.
Heat surged through him. And she wanted to be
there. Wanted him there with her and inside her
and that was the biggest turn-on of all.

But it was more than sex.

There were her shy smiles and that intent
way she would look at a part of his body before
touching it and the way she had pointed to things
under the water, her grey eyes wide with excitement. He had loved that moment of her wanting
to share something other than her body.

He loved everything about her.

He loved her.

He took a breath, trying to get his bearings.
But he felt as if he were a rowing boat without oars. He had loved Betty nine years ago but
in the intervening years his love had felt like a
weakness.

Now, though, the magnitude of what he was
feeling was impossible to deny or contain. It was
like lava pushing up, cracking him apart.

He felt Betty shift beside him, and he watched
her eyelashes flutter, his blood stirring.

'Buongiorno,' he said softly.

She opened her eyes then, and arched her
back in a stretch and he pressed his hand lightly
against her flat stomach. His heart beat loudly
as she lowered her spine back down to the mat-

tress and gazed up at him. Her grey eyes were soft and peaceful like the sky after a storm and he felt peaceful too.

'You look like a fairy-tale princess.'

'I do have some experience in that area,' she said, her hands moving to touch his face as if she found him as fascinating as he found her. 'The princess part, not the fairy tale.'

'That's something to work on, then.'

For a moment there was nothing but the sound of the sea and her shimmering grey gaze and then he leaned in and kissed her, a hot, open-mouthed kiss, and she arched upwards again.

An hour later, Betty made her way downstairs. As she caught sight of her reflection in the huge hall mirror her feet stuttered on the marble tiles. Her hair looked wild, and her eyes were huge and limpid. She looked undone. And she was, and she couldn't be happier about it.

But she told herself to be careful because she looked like a woman in love.

Mariangela beamed at her when she walked into the kitchen, and she got the distinct impression that her housekeeper knew exactly what she was thinking and feeling.

'His Grace the Duke is out in the garage, Your Highness. He said that you needed to sleep because you'd had a restless night. But he asked that you go and find him when you came down.'

'Did he?' Cheeks burning, she made her way out to the garage.

Vero was leaning over the Giulietta's engine. He turned as she walked in, and she felt her stomach flip over. There was a smudge of oil on his cheek and a smile was tugging at his mouth.

'There you are. Did you get some more rest? I told Mariangela not to wake you.'

'Yes, because I'd had a restless night. Restless!'

He grinned. 'She's Italian and a woman and she dotes on you. She wants you to have your happy ever after.'

'And that's you, is it?'

He pulled her against him and the smell of oil, and his warm skin, made her feel untethered from the ground. 'I intend to make you very happy.'

'You do make me happy,' she said, and she could have told him then that she loved him, but she would be acting on impulse and that scared her.

'And I'm about to make you happier.' Letting go of her waist, he flicked the stand and let the bonnet drop. 'I just finished changing the cam belt, so this baby is good to go.'

He held up the keys.

'Can I drive?'

He tossed them to her, then pulled open the door on the driver's side and took a step back. 'Of course, Your Highness.'

Aside from a few longish driveways and some farm tracks, there was only one road on Ponza. It bisected the island never more than a mile from the coastline. As well as only one road, there were few cars on the island. Visitors hired scooters or microcars or used the public mini-buses, so it felt as if they had gone back in time to a golden age of motoring.

'Having fun?'

Betty turned to where Vero was sitting beside her. The wind was whipping her hair in every direction and she knew her face must be flushed but she'd never felt more beautiful than when he looked at her.

He made her feel more than beautiful. Even a week ago, being seen in public like this would have felt like a revolutionary act, but she felt sure of herself and of her judgement in a way that had eluded her for so long. She could feel the change in her body too. After she and Vero split, she had felt stiff and wooden and trapped inside her skin.

But on the dance floor in Rome and moving through the clear water at Cala Gaetana and in bed with Vero, it felt as if she had woken from some hibernation. Her body no longer felt stifled and weak but strong and sure of itself.

What was more, Vero clearly liked what he saw. She could feel his gaze now and its steady intensity made her feel as if she were free falling. And he did more than look. Ever since they had gone snorkelling, he kept reaching for her, touching her face, her hair, leaning in to nip her throat or lick a path to her mouth.

And she was the same. It was as if the sea were reclaiming the land, and everything were free flowing. Remembering just how free they had been, she pressed her thighs together around the heat building there.

She felt Vero's gaze on the side of her face. Turning, she bit her lip.

'Are you really that keen to see the north of the island? We could just turn around and go back to the villa.'

'You read my mind,' he said hoarsely.

Back at the villa, they pulled off each other's clothes and then Vero nudged her into the bathroom and under the shower, spinning her around, barely waiting for her hands to press against the wet tiles before he was pushing into her, his breath shuddering against her cheek as she pressed back to meet his thrusts.

Afterwards, they made it back to the bed and he buried his face between her thighs and mapped her sensitive spots with his tongue until she jerked against his mouth, surging forward like the waves toppling against the shoreline.

They finally made it downstairs just after two for a late lunch. Vero leaned forward and speared a piece of burrata from his plate. 'Do you still want to see the cliffs?'

Putting down her cutlery, she nodded. 'But I just need to call Bella first. She's seen a horse she wants to buy and I don't want her to rush into anything.'

He smiled, one of those easy, tugging smiles that she wanted to reach out and touch.

'That's fine. I'll go and tell Gianluca our plans.' He leaned in and kissed her softly on the mouth. 'Send your sister my love.'

It was just a figure of speech, Betty thought as he strolled out of the room, but she felt hope ripple through her all the same, like a field of wheat in a summer breeze. And instead of picking up her phone, she opened her laptop. She wanted to see her sister's face.

She frowned as a melodic tune filled the room. Someone was video-calling her.

Had Bella read her mind? But it wasn't her sister. It was her grandfather.

'Nonno—how lovely. I wasn't expecting to hear from you. Is everything all right?'

Her grandfather's lined face filled the screen.

He was still a handsome man and, for all his faults, she loved him for his warmth and his enthusiasm for life and living, and for his unconditional love of her.

'I'm fine.' He waved his hand dismissively at the camera. 'Don't you worry about me. I'm just sorry I was such a clumsy fool. I so wanted to be at your wedding, but my unplanned absence was no doubt an enormous relief to your father. Probably put an actual smile on his face rather than one of those smug simpers he favours, which will improve the official photos no end.'

She laughed. 'Well, Bella and I were sorry you weren't there. Vero was too. He's so looking forward to meeting you.'

'Looking forward to it?' her grandfather repeated, his confusion adding more lines to his face. 'But we've already met. In Cairo, remember? Played a good hand at baccarat. Generous with the whisky and subbed me when I got into a spot of bother.'

Betty stared at the screen, feeling a chill spill over her face and something else, something shivery and nameless rising up from her stomach.

'I forgot, Nonno.' She smiled, but it was hard to make her lips move. Her jawbone felt as though it were wired shut. 'I've been so busy. Remind me when you met.'

'It would be a couple of months ago now. Maybe a little longer. Obviously, I knew your man had money because he was playing at the private tables. I just didn't realise how much. And then it turned out he was from Malaspina. Worked for your father. I'm a gambling man but what were the chances of that? Of him sitting down next to me?'

Probably higher than her grandfather imagined, she thought, trying to focus on breathing and smiling. But then he didn't know Vero Farnese as she did.

'And you got on?'

Her grandfather nodded. 'I liked him. He's got brains and drive. We had a good chat. I told him about the baby, and he said he was looking to get married. I said that when I told your father Nina was having a baby, he'd be in a tailspin looking for husbands for you or your sister, and then I suddenly thought, why not him? And here you are, happily married.'

He leaned in towards the screen now, his blue eyes narrowing. 'I heard von Marburg was interested in your sister, but I knew you wouldn't let her be bartered off to that old bore. I told Farnese, Betty would do anything to stop that happening.'

She stared at the screen, letting him ramble on, barely taking in a word, until finally he hung up, after promising to send her a necklace of his mother's as a wedding present.

Her head hurt. Everything hurt. Except her heart. That was numb. As if a chip of ice had pierced it and frozen it solid. And as the numbness spread, she found she couldn't move, so that she was still staring at the now blank screen when Vero walked in, the beautiful muscles of his stomach and legs moving in unison.

'You're done. That was quick. I was thinking I would have to stage an intervention. Was she okay?'

Was she okay? Was Vero really asking her that? The shocking hypocrisy and deceit of his question jerked her explosively to her feet, scraping back the chair.

'Don't do that. Don't pretend you care.'

'I do care.' He leaned back on his heels, his forehead creasing in confusion, his green eyes scanning her face. 'Why are you upset? Has something happened?'

She laughed, and then stopped because she knew if she kept laughing, she would cry and she didn't want to cry any more tears for this man. 'Yes, it has. I did it again. I made a fool of myself. I let you get under my skin and inside my head. I let myself believe you again. Trust you again. Care for you again. I laid myself bare. And all the time, you were lying.'

'I'm not lying.'

'We said we'd be honest. That we'd tell the truth.'

His hands clamped around her wrists. 'And I was, I am.'

'So why didn't you tell me you'd met my grandfather? He just called me, full of praise for you and excited to tell me about your meeting in Cairo.'

In the pause before he answered, she allowed herself to hope, to pray, to pretend, but then she saw his face and she realised that he had never stopped pretending. She just hadn't realised until now.

Vero stared at Betty, his bones heavy, his breath blistering his lungs. Around him, the walls of the room were starting to sway as if he were standing on a high, narrow ledge. It was making him feel dizzy and vertiginous and he wanted to step back. But Betty was blocking his way.

Stupid. Stupid. Stupid.

The word echoed around his head in time to the thundering of his heart. He should have told her. There had been multiple times when he could have done so. But it was never the right time. First it was too soon, then it was too hard.

And now they were here and he had no reasonable explanation except cowardice and the aforementioned stupidity.

'I was going to.'

Her eyes, Betty's beautiful eyes, flared not with anger but pain and he hated himself then, more than he had ever hated anyone.

'But you didn't. You lied.'

'I didn't—'

'By omission.' She cut across him, her disdain as terrible as the pain in her eyes. 'And why would you do that? Unless you had something to hide?'

She breathed out unsteadily. 'And you did, didn't you, Vero? Because Nonno told you everything. My dear, careless, gullible grandfather told you everything. And it would have been so easy. How you must have laughed. You plied him with drink, and you covered his debts, and you let him talk. He told you about the baby. And what my father would do when he found out. And then he told you that Hans von Marburg wanted to marry Bella and that I would do anything to stop that happening. And he was right.'

Vero was shaking his head. The skin across his cheekbones was stretched taut. 'I don't understand—'

'Then let me explain. I told my father I didn't want to marry you and he said that was fine because he had two daughters, and that if I didn't marry you Bella would have to marry Hans von Marburg.'

He felt sick to his stomach.

'I didn't know—'

'So Hans wasn't mentioned in that conversation you had with my grandfather?'

There was a beat of silence before he answered and then slowly, stiffly, he nodded. 'He was, but—' He broke off as her hand flew up to cover her mouth.

'Betty, I'm sorry.'

Her eyes were filled with shock and disbelief.

'She's twenty years old.'

'I know. But I didn't know that your father would do that.'

'Nonno told you that I'd do anything to stop that happening. Why did you think I married you?'

His eyes flared. 'The same reason you do everything. To please your father. To earn his approval and protect the House of Marchetta. That's all you've ever cared about.'

'And you only care about yourself. You're ruthless and selfish. Self-serving.'

'Yes, maybe in the beginning I was all those things. I wanted to punish you and my father—'

'And I understood that. But you were also ready for Bella to be punished too.' There was a sheen of tears in her eyes. 'You need to leave.'

'I can't. I can't leave because I love you, Betty.' There was a shake to his voice, and an hour earlier those three words would have made her heart sing and her life complete. But it was just another lie designed to manipulate her. She felt suddenly, incredibly tired.

'You do that so well. I can see why you've been so successful. You make it sound so true and you can keep lying to yourself if you want but what you're talking about is lust.'

'I'm not lying to you or myself. I do love you. And I think you love me. So let's work this through.' He yanked a chair out from the table. 'Let's sit down and talk. Look, I know I messed up but I was a different person then. You were different too. But we changed, we grew together, not apart. That's the truth. Our truth. You have to believe me, Betty. Believe in me, in us. That's all I want. I don't care about the title. I don't want to be your prince. I want to be your husband—'

He was looking at her as if she were standing on a window ledge and he were reaching out with his hand. And it would be so easy to just lean forward and take it, and let herself be drawn back in.

But then it would get so much more difficult, and painful, even more painful than this.

She nodded slowly.

'You're right. I am a different person. For so long, I tried to be the perfect princess. To make my parents love me. But I'm done with that. Because perfect isn't just the enemy of good, it's the enemy of happy too, and I want to be happy. I want a divorce.'

For a split second, she saw something flare then fade in his eyes and the pain of it almost robbed her of the power of speech, but she had to do this. She couldn't take his hand, couldn't take a chance.

'But you can keep your title so you can be happy too. That's all you ever wanted anyway.'

'I haven't been wearing a condom. You could be pregnant.' His voice was so devoid of emotion it took her a moment to take in what he had said.

'And this is what you want to bring your child into? A life of lies and deceit. I don't understand you, Vero. I thought that was what you hated.'

He stared at her in silence and then his mouth pulled into the saddest smile she had ever seen. 'I did hate it. And you're right, our child deserves better than that. You deserve better. You deserve a man you can trust and love. A man who doesn't make you pretend. A man who you're proud to call your husband. Don't let anyone ever tell you differently. Whatever it takes, don't settle for anything less.'

There was a strange, shifting light in his eyes, and his breathing wasn't quite steady. For a moment she thought he was going to say something else and then he turned and strode out of the room without a backward glance.

Anxiety and panic ripped through her and for a frantic moment, Betty was tempted to run after him. But there was no point. Her judgement was flawed. That was the only truth and, sitting down on the chair that Vero had pulled out moments earlier, she started to weep.

CHAPTER TEN

WALKING BACK THROUGH the villa and out onto the terrace, Vero felt as if everyone were watching him. Although the opposite was true. Mari-angela had smiled stiffly then glanced away and Bianca, one of the maids, had actually reversed back into the kitchen through the doorway.

He doubted they had heard much. Betty's pain and his guilt for causing that pain had directed his anger and despair inwards so that he had barely raised his voice. And Betty had got quieter and quieter as if her voice wanted to shrink back inside her. In the same way she had wrapped her arms around her waist to hold herself close.

He had hated that, hated that she was so closed off to him. Even more so than when she had been on the other side of the world.

Then he'd had his anger to warm him, to give him purpose, to drive his days. Now he couldn't think of how he was going to live the rest of his life without her.

He had reached the steps leading down to the jetty, and for a moment, he stopped at the top.

But he was going to have to find a way because Betty didn't want him. She wanted a divorce.

The word and its implications made his breath stutter, his feet too, so that he almost lost his balance and had to reach for the handrail to steady himself.

A life without Betty. A life without her warm, eager body straddling him. A life without that smile, not the public princess smile but the one that made her grey eyes turn silver and dance like raindrops on the surface of a lake. A life without her face tilted up expectantly towards his as they talked and laughed.

It tore into him then and the need to see her again was like the dragging, inexorable pull of the moon on the tide, and he wanted to turn back.

He would tell her that she couldn't have a divorce. That he wouldn't agree. He would make her sit down, make her listen, make her agree to what he wanted.

And then what?

Wasn't that what he'd already done? And it had crushed her, he thought, picturing her small, trembling body and the way she was trying to hold it all in, hold herself together, not trying to be the perfect princess but a woman trying not to break.

No, he couldn't go back. He couldn't force her to stay with him. It would crush her, hurt her again and even more than he'd already hurt her.

There was an ache in his chest that came from not knowing when, if, he would see her again. But he let himself feel the pain. If he loved her, and he did with every breath and bone in his body, then he had to leave. He had to accept her choice.

He stepped up onto the yacht. Gianluca glanced up from where he was talking to one of the crew.

'We're leaving,' he said to him quietly. 'I'll be in my cabin.'

Gianluca nodded, then hesitated. '*Sì*, Signor Farnese… I mean, Your Grace. But which course shall I set?'

Vero shrugged. 'I don't care. Just sail for the horizon.'

It didn't matter where he went because he would be going without Betty, and anywhere would be nowhere without her.

Thirty minutes had passed since Vero had left but Betty could still feel his presence in the room. And probably she always would. He had left scars and watching him walk through that door was the hardest thing she had ever done. But it was for the best.

Her hand moved to press her stomach. Best for everyone. Even Vero.

He didn't love her.

In their entire time together, he had never once mentioned love until today. Need, in its most primal sense. But that wasn't love. It was lust and she had thought briefly that it might be enough for them. That urgent, sweet, encompassing, humbling hunger they felt for one another.

'*Scusi*, Your Highness?'

Betty glanced up. Mariangela was standing in the doorway with a tray. 'Yes? Sorry, did I order some tea?'

'No, Your Highness. But His Royal Highness Prince Frederico always took tea when he needed to calm his mind.'

'I remember.' Betty cleared her throat. Nonno had picked up the habit during one of his early love affairs in London. 'That's very kind of you, Mariangela.'

The housekeeper smiled. 'Just ring the bell if you need anything, Your Highness.'

But she wouldn't need to, Betty thought as she picked up the teapot and poured out a cup. Mariangela always knew what was needed before any bell was rung. If only she had the same sixth sense. Maybe none of this would have happened.

Or maybe it would. There was something there with Vero, something that transcended time and distance. A tiny shimmering thread that had refused to break for all those years. It had straddled the globe, criss-crossing America and the Middle East and Europe and it should have snapped or snarled into knots like the necklaces that Bella used to bring to her to untangle when she was little.

Only what should have weakened or damaged it had made it stronger.

It had stayed strong and straight and true, surviving their anger and distrust and the high-pressure spectacle of a royal wedding. And they had both fought it. Furiously. But in the middle of all that fury and frustration they had met in the middle.

They had talked and listened. They hadn't sat in judgement or walked away. She thought back to Vero sleeping on the sofa in her bedroom, his big body contorted against the cushions.

He had stayed there all night. And then he had magicked up his yacht and taken her out on the ocean, sensing, knowing, that the freedom and the fluidity of the water were what she'd needed most.

But that wasn't all he had done. Afterwards, he had surprised her by taking her to Rome and they had spent the rest of the day being Betty and Vero. Shopping, eating, dancing, like any normal couple in love.

And then, they had made love.

Her chest felt as if it were about to burst open. Because it wasn't just sex for Vero. He loved her.

And she could spend the rest of her life doubting that, doubting herself, but she knew she was right.

It took her seven minutes to run, no, sprint, to the jetty. But as she reached the top of the steps, her legs slowed.

The yacht was gone. Vero was gone.

She felt a knot in her throat. She was too late. And she had lost him again. She had no idea where to look or how to find him.

But there had to be a way. Her brain scrambled through the possibilities. There was one. It would mean asking Mariangela for help.

She turned and stopped. Mariangela was walking down the steps. Smiling, she held out her phone. 'I hope you don't mind, Your Highness, but I took the liberty of calling my cousin.'

Reaching for the whisky bottle, Vero unscrewed the cap and sloshed a finger-width into a glass. He was taking his time, letting the alcohol seep slowly through his blood rather than drinking it straight from the bottle as he had the last time Betty and he had broken up. But this time he needed to keep feeling the pain, her pain, otherwise he knew he'd be tempted to order Gianluca to turn the yacht around.

So he was drinking just enough to take the edge off, and hopefully he would be far enough into the ocean by the time the bottle was empty, and Betty would have spoken to her father and there would be another reason to add to the list of things that would keep them apart for ever.

There was a knock on the cabin door and he ran his hand over his face.

'I told you I don't care where we go,' he shouted, without getting up from his desk.

The door inched open and one of the crew stepped into the crack, looking nervous. 'I'm sorry to bother you, Your Grace—'

'Don't call me that.'

'Yes, Your— I mean, Signor Farnese. It's not about the course, sir. The captain has asked that you come on deck.'

'I'm sure I'm not needed.'

'Unfortunately, you are. The coastguard has pulled us over and they want to speak to the owner.'

Vero shut his eyes briefly. The last thing he needed right now was to have to deal with some officious jobsworth, but the Guardia Costiera were essentially the police at sea.

As he stepped out on deck, the sunlight made him blink so that for a moment he only saw the men in their dark uniforms.

'I'm Vero Farnese. What seems to be the problem?'

The coastguard cleared his throat. 'There is no problem, Your Grace.'

He frowned. 'Then might I ask what you're doing on my boat?'

And then he saw her.

Her.

He almost lost his footing and suddenly it was a struggle to stop the air leaking from his lungs.

She was standing slightly to one side, her hand resting on the rail as it had done only days ago when he had leaned in to kiss her throat. But she couldn't be real. He stared at the woman in the striped sundress in confusion. He must be hallucinating. But he had only drunk one glass of whisky.

And then she stepped forward and he knew instantly that he wasn't dreaming. Knew from the way every nerve ending in his body tightened and the sense of loss stabbing beneath his ribs. And because of that hair. Nobody had hair like Betty. Right now, it was tied loosely with a scarf, and he would have given every share in his company to reach out and touch those rippling auburn curls.

'I asked these gentlemen if they might give me a lift and they very kindly agreed to drop me off,' she said into the shifting silence on deck, in that quiet, clear way of hers that made his stomach perform a low, swooping loop. Just as if the coastguard were her chauffeur and she were going to a garden party.

'You did?'

Just seeing her again made him feel tender and bruised inside.

She nodded, then turned towards the assembled men in their uniforms 'I think I can take it from here. But thank you very much for your help.'

Vero watched the coastguards return to their boat. There was a sudden, loud rasping sound as the engine started that faded as the boat accelerated across the water and all that remained then was the slap of the waves against the yacht's hull. It wasn't just the coastguards who had disappeared, he realised a moment later. His crew had vanished too.

Now it was just him and Betty and all the things he wanted to give to her and needed back, but which she was incapable of reciprocating.

'What are you doing here, Betty?' he said finally.

'I realised after you left that I had left some important things unsaid. About the future.'

The tiny fluttering shoot of hope that he had been ignoring at the margins of his brain withered and died. So she just wanted to talk about the divorce.

'Of course. What is it that you want to say?'

'That I'm sorry—'

He stared at her in appalled silence. The last few days she had grown in confidence and now he had set her back, crushed her again.

'You don't need to apologise to me, I should be the one apologising to you.'

'And you did. But I wouldn't accept it.'

She sounded vulnerable, but then he realised that she was showing him her vulnerability as proof of her trust.

'I didn't want to. I was angry and upset so I did what you did. I lashed out. I hurt the person I love, because I know you love me, Vero, and I love you, and I didn't say it before, and that's what I'm sorry for. For not being honest. But you were right. I do love you. I've only ever loved you.'

'And I've only ever loved you.' Reaching out, he pulled her into his arms.

Betty leaned into him, breathing out unsteadily.

'That's why I came after you. You told me not to settle for anything less than a man I can trust and love. A man who wouldn't make me pretend, who I was proud to call my husband. And I am proud of you, Vero, so very proud and happy to be your wife.'

Her face was soft and open, and he felt her love for him in his bones.

'I can't believe you got the coastguard to pick you up.'

'I didn't know how to find you but then Mariangela called her cousin for me. He's a coastguard down by Naples and he knew who to call.

They patrol all the time, so they came to the jetty to pick me up.'

'What did you say to them?'

She screwed up her face. 'I told them we'd had an argument. And that I'd said some things I didn't mean. And that my husband had said some things he did mean. But that we loved each other and that I needed their help so that we could find our way back to each other.'

He stared at her incredulously. 'You do realise this is going to be all over the Internet by tonight.'

'Why do you think I wore this dress?'

He laughed then. 'Your father is going to lose his mind.'

'He'll get over it. But I would never get over losing you.'

His arm tightened around her. 'I meant what I said. I don't care about the title.'

She kissed him softly on the mouth. 'I don't care about it either. It doesn't matter at all because you're a prince among men to me, and more importantly you're the love of my life.'

'I love you, Betty,' he said, leaning in and kissing her slowly, and then, scooping her into his arms, he carried her across the deck and down the companionway to his cabin and to their future.

* * * * *

HARLEQUIN
Reader Service

Enjoyed your book?

Try the perfect subscription for Romance readers and get more great books like this delivered right to your door.

See why over 10+ million readers have tried Harlequin Reader Service.

Start with a Free Welcome Collection with free books and a gift—valued over $20.

Choose any series in print or ebook. See website for details and order today:

   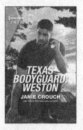

TryReaderService.com/subscriptions